Secret
IN THE
Willows

SummerHill Secrets

Whispers Down the Lane
Secret in the Willows

SECRET
IN THE
WILLOWS

Beverly Lewis

BETHANY HOUSE PUBLISHERS
MINNEAPOLIS, MINNESOTA 55438

Cover illustration by Chris Ellison

Published by Bethany House Publishers
A Ministry of Bethany Fellowship, Inc.
11300 Hampshire Avenue South
Minneapolis, Minnesota 55438

Printed in the United States of America.

Library of Congress Cataloging-in-Publication Data

Lewis, Beverly
   Secret in the Willows / Beverly Lewis.
      p.   cm. — (SummerHill secrets ; 2)
   Summary: After Merry befriends Elton, an artistically talented
boy whom some of her eighth grade classmates call retarded, she
must find a way to prove that he is not responsible for the damage
at the farm of her Amish friend, Rachel.

   [1. Mentally handicapped—Fiction. 2. Christian life—Fiction.
3. Amish—Fiction.] I. Title. II. Series: Lewis, Beverly, 1949–
SummerHill secrets ; 2.
PZ7.L58464Sdh   1994
[Fic]—dc20   95–1260
ISBN 1–55661–477–2   CIP
                                                 AC

To Charette
Thanks for many things.
Best of all—
friendship.

We cannot tell the precise moment when friendship is formed. As in filling a vessel drop by drop, there is at last a drop which makes it run over; so in a series of kindnesses there is at last one which makes the heart run over.

—Samuel Johnson

ONE

It was one of those soggy springtime mornings when nothing goes right. First off, I slept through my alarm, which led to another problem: My hair.

Flat and fringy, my shoulder-length locks only looked good curled. To give the illusion of more body, I always added a leave-in conditioner. Today there was no time for that ritual. And to make things worse, just as I was turning on the only curling iron-in-residence, it coughed up smoke and died.

"Mom!" I shrieked.

My brother Skip poked his head into my room. "What's all the noise? Lose a cat?" He cast an older-brother sneer at me and snapped up his high school letter jacket.

"Like you really care." I shook the defunct curl-maker, pulled the cord out, and plugged it right back in again. No little red light. No heat. No use.

Skip spied the problem and laughed. "Maybe you oughta call that friend of yours, uh, Chelsea Davis, the girl with all the great hair."

"And why don't you just disappear," I retorted. But

9

instead of leaving, Skip inched farther into my room.

"Mom!" I yelled even louder.

Skip mumbled some unintelligible comment about my room smelling like kitty litter. Just then, Shadrach, Meshach, and Abednego, my three courageous cats, bounded off the bed toward him. Skip spun around and raced down the hall with a trail of hissing felines at his heels.

Served him right.

At last, Mom arrived on the scene. She surveyed my stringy hair, then checked out the dead curling iron with an audible sigh. Reaching for a yellow scrunchie, Mom began to pull my hair back. "How about a ponytail today, Merry?"

"Mom, please," I whined. "I'm going to school."

"You're absolutely right," she said, still holding my limp hair. "But I have a wonderful idea."

I cringed. "Wha-a-t?"

"Since you're stuck wearing your hair straight and flat today, let's not have it hug your head too much."

"Like how?" I glanced at my watch. "We really don't have time for a total remake here, Mom. The bus comes in exactly eighteen and a half minutes."

She marched into my bathroom expecting me to follow. Reluctantly, I did. She filled her palm with mousse and began applying it to my flimsy hair.

I groaned.

"Trust me, Merry Hanson," and the way she said it sounded exactly like me. I leaned down while she flipped my hair over my face. Next, she turned on the blow dryer, high heat. "This'll help seal in the shine," she said over the noise.

I had an instant vision of Marcia Brady from *The Brady Bunch*, wearing her linear locks center-parted and slightly greasy. "Uh . . . Mom . . . not too shiny, okay?"

While bent over, I stuffed my nubby yellow shirt inside my denim, bib-topper jumper outfit. The tomboy look had recently become a big deal at Mifflin Middle School. I, however, had always felt comfortable in casual wear like this. At last the fashion trend was swinging my way.

When my hair was completely dry, I flipped it back over my head. Mom wanted to help brush it out, but she'd done enough. I moved closer to the mirror. "Not bad," I said. "Thanks, Mom."

Downstairs at breakfast, Skip pretended not to notice my super straight look. Mom's strong kitchen presence always helped bring on spurts of Skip's most civilized behavior. She gave me a second piece of toast to go with my scrambled eggs, and piled it high with homemade strawberry jam from the Zooks, our Amish neighbors down the lane.

Before leaving the house, I rechecked my hair, spraying it lightly. That done, I set off down SummerHill Lane to wait for the school bus near the willow grove. Abednego and his feline brothers scampered after me.

Wild strawberry vines, glistening with April morning dew, graced the grassy slopes on either side of the dirt road. It was a misty Pennsylvania morning, complete with thunder. I almost went back to the house for an umbrella, but I could see the bus topping the hill in the distance.

In the opposite direction, I spotted Rachel Zook, my Amish friend, walking barefooted with her younger sisters, Nancy, Susie, and Ella Mae. Aaron, that rascal brother of theirs, ran ahead as if daring one of them to catch him. They were headed for the one-room school the Amish kids attended in this part of Lancaster County.

Rachel stopped, turning to wave as her long green dress and black apron billowed out softly in the warm spring breeze. "Good morning, Merry!" she called, her bookbag bumping against her dress.

I was too far away to see the permanent twinkle in her blue eyes, but I was sure it was there.

"Come on over after school, *jah?*" she called again.

Something was wrong. The cheerful ring was missing from Rachel's voice.

"Everything okay?" I asked, hurrying to catch up with her. She cast a cautious eye on the younger kids and shook her head.

"What is it, Rachel?" I asked. "What's wrong?"

She raised a finger to her lips. Her eyes looked suddenly gray as she stared at me. "Not now," she whispered fearfully. "I mustn't talk now."

I touched her arm. "I'll be right over after school, okay?"

She nodded, avoiding my eyes just then, and I knew something was dreadfully wrong.

Rachel ran ahead to catch up with her brother and three sisters without offering her usual goodbye wave. I turned back toward the willow grove to wait for the bus, worried.

Thunder gave way to pelting rain, and the Zook children scurried down the lane splashing their bare feet against the muddy road. Rachel and little Susie opened their umbrellas and Aaron balanced his lunch box on top of his straw hat. My cats scampered home to safety as another thunderbolt boomed overhead. As for keeping my hair dry, I tried to protect it with my schoolbag. So much for my fluffy-but-straight hairdo.

I thought about Rachel's plain Amish hairstyle while I waited for the slowpoke bus. She never had to fuss with things like curling irons or hair spray. Her long hair, like that of all other Amish women, was simply parted down the middle, pulled into a bun at the back of her head, and never cut. Since there was no electricity in Amish homes, it was the easy way.

Just when the cloudburst threatened to destroy my entire look, the bus showed up. I climbed onto the noisy school bus searching for Chelsea Davis. My friend was nowhere to be seen, so I scooted into the nearest available seat.

The bus lurched forward, and I could see the Zook kids up ahead. Rachel was trudging along, head down and bookbag dragging. I leaned against the window, watching until I could see her no longer. Rachel's dark mood made my heart pound. She was usually so cheerful.

What could be wrong?

TWO

By the time I arrived at school, my hair had begun to dry out. At least *some* things were improving.

I pit-stopped at my locker on my race to art class. Students were slamming locker doors and shouting at each other in the hallway while I scrounged through the junk in my locker, searching for my sketch pad.

That's when it happened.

In the midst of the noisy scrambling, a creepy sensation sat on the back of my neck. Like someone was staring at me. Really staring. Gooseprickles crawled up my scalp, but I kept facing the locker, determined not to turn around.

Someone's eyes were boring a hole in the back of my head. And I was pretty sure who it was.

Jonathan Klein.

Tall with light brown hair and brown eyes that matched mine, Jon was the one guy at school I secretly loved. In reality, Jon Klein was the one and only guy on the planet that I could even begin to think of in terms of the M word.

Only one question remained: When would he come

to his senses and notice I was girlfriend material? Jon and I did have one thing going for us—the Alliteration Game. It was a word game he had initiated months ago, and I surprised him by meeting the challenge. Anyway, it was a private, very special thing between us. At least from my point of view.

Say it with all p's, Jon would say, each day choosing a specific letter of the alphabet. And we'd go off doing our word thing, the Alliteration Wizard and I.

Today, however, Jon was silent behind me. Simply staring. I stuffed my sketch pad into my schoolbag and grabbed my books for morning classes. The uneasy feeling continued. Why wasn't he making his usual crazy comments?

I waited another second, scarcely breathing. What would it be like for him to carry my books? Was he going to ask me today?

A brilliant idea flashed through my brain. Quickly, I reached for my camera. Taking pictures, good pictures, was my main hobby in life. My camera accompanied me everywhere. Everywhere and always.

Swallowing a giggle, I took the lens cap off, keeping the camera close to my body until just the right moment. Wouldn't Jon be surprised when I took an unposed shot of him?

Like right . . . about . . .

Now! I spun around. *Click!*

Light exploded, surprising my subject. His hands flew to his face, shielding his eyes. I lowered the camera and gasped as I realized my mistake. Across the hall from me, Elton Keel, a special-needs student, stood dazed.

This is truly horrible, I thought as I left my locker and hurried over to him. His arms still covered his face as I sputtered out my apologies. His hair was short and blond, the color of sweet corn, and he wore a blue and red plaid backpack.

"I . . . I'm really sorry," I said again, waiting for the boyish face to emerge out of hiding. Slowly, he lowered his arms, letting them hang at his side. They seemed too long for the rest of his body.

"You okay?" I asked.

Elton nodded his head emphatically; kept nodding again and again. Then he stopped abruptly and looked down at his shirt pocket, pulling on it. With a little grunt, he grasped the tip of a blue ink pen and brought it up out of his pocket, displaying it proudly.

I still felt lousy about startling him with my flash. "Really, I thought you were someone else."

He didn't answer and I didn't expect him to. Everyone knew Elton Keel didn't speak; at least no one had heard him say anything since he transferred here.

He started clicking his ball-point pen. Fast. On and off. On. Off. Over and over, like the monotonous ticking of a clock. I'd heard about Elton's quirks and rituals. But this . . .

"Hey, Merry!"

I turned to see Chelsea. Her sea-green eyes sparkled as she flew down the hall. Her auburn hair floated like a curtain around her.

"Hi," I said, taking a little step back from Elton. "Did ya miss the bus?"

"Mom drove me. She had a bunch of errands."

Chelsea looked at my flat hair. "Get caught in the rain, Mer?" Before I could answer she pulled a tan corduroy newsboy cap out of her schoolbag. "Here, try this."

She plopped it on my head.

"Thanks," I said.

She grinned. "Stunning." And just like that she was off without so much as a glance at Elton.

I looked at my watch and at Elton still standing there. "It's time for first hour. You coming?"

He leaned his head down as if he wanted to listen to my watch. I held my arm out. "It doesn't make sounds," I said, feeling slightly awkward about having Elton's head so close. But the embarrassment didn't last. He stood up and started clicking his pen again. I turned back to my locker to put my camera away.

Without warning, Elton began grunting in a sort of high-pitched way. I turned to investigate and saw that he had jerked his backpack around and was pulling out his sketch pad, holding it high.

"Oh, you think you're gonna be late for art?" I said. "Well, so am I. Let's go!"

We made our way through the chaotic maze of students together. It felt a little strange walking with Elton to class, but I ignored the weird looks from other students as they dodged first him and then me.

Weird looks aside, it was impossible to miss the rude stares as we entered art class. Several guys whooped and hollered as Elton held the door for me. I glanced over my shoulder, wondering how much of the ridicule Elton had absorbed. He was cherub-faced, without the smile, and his eyes looked dull, almost lifeless. Kids like Elton experienced the same emotions as everyone else, I'd been told. Their emotions just didn't register in the eyes. I knew this from hearing my dad talk about several of his hospital patients.

A quick look around Mrs. Hawkins' art room told me she hadn't arrived yet. So I made a big deal about thanking Elton, staring especially hard at Cody Gower, one of the roughest kids in school.

"Hey, looks like Merry's got herself a new man," Cody taunted. A bunch of guys joined him with whistles and laughter. I felt truly sorry for Elton, but he didn't seem to mind.

The bell rang and Mrs. Hawkins showed up wearing her usual array of colorful bangles and beads. Before sitting down, she glanced at her seating chart. She made no comment about Elton's choice of seating—the empty desk directly across from mine.

I got right to work refining my charcoal sketch. Unlike some students who'd elected art as a sluff course, I enjoyed the class. Besides that, I valued Mrs. Hawkins' expert input.

Someone else was an expert in the class. Cody Gower. His expertise had nothing to do with art, though. Cody was a natural at stirring up trouble.

I concentrated on my project, taking time to shade in my charcoal sketch of an old covered bridge—Hunsecker's Mill Bridge—which I'd photographed many times. The 180-foot bridge crossed the Conestoga River not far from my house. I knew it was really old, built in 1848. Rachel Zook called it the Kissing Bridge because it was where her big brother, Curly John, stole his first kiss from Sarah—now his bride.

I stopped working long enough to blow some fine gray dust off my paper. As I did, Cody got up and stood in the aisle beside Elton's desk. Definitely up to no good.

Where was Mrs. Hawkins? I leaned up out of my seat and scanned the classroom. She was gone—again! Probably called out while I was deep in thought, working on my project.

"Cody! Leave him alone," I demanded, suddenly attracting the attention of the whole class.

Cody ignored me and picked up Elton's sketch, inspecting it. "Is this your work?" he asked in a friendly yet mocking tone.

Elton nodded, wearing a vacant stare. Over and over he nodded. A rush of whispers and giggles rose from the room mixed with the unmistakable sound of "retard."

I sucked in a breath and held it till I nearly burst. Elton, on the other hand, seemed calm enough. Poor guy. I had to find a way to help.

Cody leaned down, studying Elton. "Mind if I show the others?" he asked, casting repulsive smirks at the class like a fly-fisherman throwing out his line.

"Yeah, let's see the retard's masterpiece!" shouted one boy. That was all it took to lead the pack of shouting maniacs.

I leaped out of my seat. "Give me that!" I yelled, lunging for Elton's art.

"Stay out of this," Cody sneered, but I grabbed the sketch out of his hand anyway.

"No, you sit down, Cody Gower. You don't wanna

mess up your grade in here, do you?" It was a threat, but I couldn't help it. Everyone knew why Cody had signed up for this class—an easy A.

"C'mon, Merry. Show us the picture!" called one of Cody's friends.

I ignored the pleas to exhibit Elton's work. Still standing, I deliberately placed his sketch facedown on my desk. As for Cody, he had no choice but to comply with my demand, because at that moment, Mrs. Hawkins waltzed into the room.

I sat down and handed Elton's drawing back to him. He started working on it as if nothing had happened.

The girl behind me tapped my shoulder. "Good going, Merry," she whispered.

I made a thumbs-up gesture without turning around. Mrs. Hawkins, meanwhile, started moving from one desk to another. She didn't get far, though, because the bell rang.

I stayed at my desk until everyone left. Elton sat too, off in another world, oblivious to the bell and the noisy mass exodus. I leaned forward to get his attention, pointing to his drawing. "Is it okay with you if I take a look?"

He began his nodding ritual.

Curiously, I studied the picture on his desk. It was a near-perfect, ink-drawn sketch of a girl. I glanced over at his ball-point pen dangling between two fingers. Whoever heard of doing sketches with a pen! No second chances like with pencil, yet in Elton's case it appeared that no erasures were needed. "It's genius," I whispered. "How'd you do this?"

Elton stared blankly at the drawing, and for an instant

I thought I saw the corners of his mouth twitch. Clutching his pen, he began to nod again. He clicked his pen on and off and stopped. Was he trying to communicate with me? It was then that I noticed a faint brightness in his normally empty eyes.

I gazed at his sketch again. What lines—what style!

Suddenly, with an uncontrolled, jerking motion, he wrote: *4 U* at the bottom and handed the picture to me.

"I can't take your work, Elton. You'll be getting a grade for this—a terrific grade!" I traced my finger around the soft, full curls of the girl's shoulder-length hair; noticed the bright eyes.

Then it hit me—the girl he'd drawn wasn't just any girl.

Elton Keel's art project was a sketch of me!

THREE

"I've never seen anything like it," I told Chelsea as we waited for the bus after school. "Elton Keel sketches with a ball-point pen."

"So?"

"He gets it right the first time," I insisted. "Nobody does that." I went on to tell her about the drawing he'd made of me.

She pulled her hair back over one shoulder, smiling. "Where's the drawing now?"

"I gave it back to him."

"Oh, that's just great," she said. "He's probably depressed. Don't you know anything about retards?"

My blood boiled. "Don't say that!"

"What's *your* problem?"

"You're wrong," I heard myself saying. "He's not that . . . that word you said. Elton's a person. A very special and totally gifted person!"

Chelsea didn't say anything. She just looked at me. And when the bus came, we climbed on in silence.

"God created each of us with unique gifts," I said, settling into our regular spot close to the front. "You make straight *A*'s consistently, and I see beauty in nature and photograph it, and Elton . . . well, you know . . ."

Chelsea frowned, scooting back and pushing her knees up against the seat in front of us. "You're not going to launch off on one of your Bible stories now, are you?"

It's no use, I thought, glancing over my shoulder at Lissa Vyner, another one of my school friends. She was sitting and laughing in the back of the bus with Ashley Horton, our new pastor's daughter, and several other kids from my church, including Jon Klein. I watched Lissa for a moment. She seemed so much more settled—happier, too, since her dad was in therapy. Lissa and her mom had started coming to church nearly every Sunday.

I sighed. *Why can't Chelsea be more like Lissa? Why does she fight me every time I talk about God?*

Chelsea poked my arm. "Hello-o?" she taunted. "Wanna go back and sit with the Christians?" She nodded her head in the direction of Lissa, Jon, and friends.

"Please, Chelsea," I said, "don't do this."

She slapped her hand down hard on her history book. "Well, then don't preach."

I wanted to tell her to stop hiding her head in the sand. To open her eyes to God. But I knew better than to push things.

❧ ❧

At home, I dropped off my books, eager to see Rachel Zook. I ran down SummerHill Lane, turned, and took the shortcut through the willow grove to the Amish farmhouse. The house was set back off the main road with a white picket fence circling the pasture area. There were empty fruit jars turned upside down all along the fence for storage, a sure proof that Rachel and her mother expected an abundant crop of garden vegetables. All around me, rich and moist Lancaster County soil was ready for spring planting.

I noticed Abe Zook and Levi, his sixteen-year-old son, out on the front porch repairing a window. Abe stopped working and straightened up. Levi's eyes lit up when he saw me. Silly boy. When would he ever give up his crazy notion of taking me riding in his courting buggy?

Levi's father smiled a greeting and scratched his long, untrimmed beard as I came up the front porch. I hated to think what would happen if Abe Zook knew that Levi had taken a more-than-friendly interest in me. Amish were supposed to date among themselves. Even casual dating of "English"—the term they used for non-Amish—was not allowed. It was a fearful thing to be reprimanded by the bishop. And far worse if the baptized person continued in rebellion. A shunning was sure to follow.

Levi swept up the shattered glass scattered over the front porch. When his father wasn't looking he tipped his hat at me, grinning.

"What on earth happened here?" I asked.

Levi started to explain, but Abe touched his son's shoulder, shaking his head solemnly. It was clear enough to me: someone had thrown a brick through the Zooks' living room window. But since the Amish were peace-loving folk, the police would never know about it.

"Merry!" Rachel called to me from inside the house. "Come on in. I've been waiting for you."

My friend wasn't exactly sitting around twiddling her thumbs. She was helping her mother with spring cleaning. And by the looks of things, it was a day to scour the tinware—loaf pans, cookie sheets, and pie pans.

Rachel went to wash her hands at the sink before joining me. "*Es gookt verderbt schee doh,*" she said. "It looks mighty nice here."

I smiled, agreeing with her. One thing for sure, the Zooks liked to have things sparkling and clean.

"Come on out to the barn," Rachel said, drying her hands on a corner of her black apron. There was a look of apprehension in her eyes.

I followed her through the large kitchen; the gray painted walls looked bare without pictures. Not a single border of wallpaper or a lacy white curtain graced the monotonous walls. A tan oilcloth covered the table with a royal blue place mat at its center. On it, a square glass dish held rooster and hen salt and pepper shakers and a white sugar bowl. Plain, but clean, the Zook home was always one of my favorite places.

Outside, Rachel's younger sisters stirred up a cloud of dust as they swept the back steps and sidewalk. I stopped to talk to Nancy and Ella Mae, but Rachel ignored the girls and made a beeline around the barn.

The Zooks' barn was called a "bank barn" because an earthen ramp had been built on one side leading to the second floor. The ramp made it possible to store additional farm equipment since the upper-level doors opened to the dirt ramp.

Rachel stood at the top of the ramp, motioning for me

to hurry. "I can't be long. Dat and Levi need help with the milking."

I knew the Zooks started afternoon milking around four, so I ran to catch up with my friend.

"Someone is trying to hurt us," she said softly, her eyes more serious than I'd ever seen them. She leaned against the wide barn door.

"Are you talking about the broken window?"

She nodded solemnly, much the way her father had before. "Someone is mighty angry." She paused, peering into the barn where the second story was divided into sections of feed bins, haymows, and two threshing floors. Then her voice became a whisper. "Very bad things are going on around here, Merry."

I stared at Rachel. "What else?"

"Tuesday a hate letter came in the mail, and yesterday someone let Apple out of the barn."

"Did you find your horse?"

"Dat and Levi found her near the Conestoga River. They looked all around everywhere outside and never did find out who let her out." She tucked a strand of light brown hair into the bun at the back of her neck. "You know what I think? I think one of Jake Fisher's boys is mad at us."

Now I was really curious. "Old Jake has *six* boys."

"But only one of them caught trouble with the Lancaster bishops." She studied me hard. "If you promise you won't tell anyone, I'll say what happened."

"I'll keep it quiet. I promise."

Rachel stepped close to me, eager to divulge her secret about the Amish family down the lane.

 # FOUR

"I think Ben Fisher's the one causing trouble," Rachel whispered. "Dat caught him out joyriding with a carload of 'English' girls. After being baptized and all, Ben made no bones about it. Didn't even say he was sorry."

"Your father saw him for sure?"

"Jah." Rachel nodded. "Worse than that, Dat found out Ben Fisher owns that car!" Cars were forbidden for life, among the Old Order Amish.

Just last fall Ben had made a vow to follow the rules of the *Ordnung*—the blueprint for being Amish. At his baptism, he would have been told it was far better to never make his vow than to make it and break it later.

Rachel continued. "My father told our deacon about it, and the church members had a meeting with the bishops. From what I heard, Ben Fisher didn't go along with a kneeling confession for driving a car. And he wasn't just a little huffy when he stormed out of the meeting."

"Do you think Ben will confess?"

"The bishops gave him six weeks to do it, but the time's already half up." Rachel's eyes were bright with sudden tears. "Oh, Merry, he's one of Levi's best friends, and he's in danger of the *Meidung*—the shunning!"

I put my arm around Rachel. "You okay?"

"I'm afraid for Ben Fisher," she cried. "The shunning is awful!" Rachel leaned her head against mine. "None of us can talk to him or eat with him if he's shunned, and it can last for a lifetime unless—"

"Don't worry," I said, comforting her. "Maybe he'll come back and repent."

She wiped her eyes. "If only Levi could talk sense into Ben . . . before he does something real terrible."

Shunning was something I didn't fully understand, but I knew it meant being cut off from the people you knew and loved. Like being disowned.

I followed Rachel through the hayloft and climbed down the ladder to the lower level. Cows shuffled into the barn, some mooing loudly as they slapped their tails, swishing flies away. Like clockwork, the herd headed for the milking stalls, twenty-four strong.

I wondered how strong an influence Levi might be on Ben Fisher. If Ben didn't repent and sell his car, Levi could lose his friend forever. "Does your father think Ben's the one who threw the brick?" I asked.

Rachel raised a finger to her lips and wiped her eyes, shielding them as her father entered the barn. He set down clanking milk buckets in preparation for the afternoon milking. "No one in the house talks about it, and neither must you," she said, reminding me of my promise.

"You can count on me," I replied firmly.

The next day was Friday and the school cafeteria was bustling with noise. Everyone seemed wired for the weekend. And the closer to summer we got, the harder it was to concentrate on school.

I was settled in at a table, leaning back in my chair while I ate a tuna sandwich. Chelsea and Lissa sat with me, having hot lunch. Elton Keel sat three tables behind us. He was holding a hamburger in one hand and, with the other, clicking his pen to beat the band.

Chelsea noticed me watching him. "I wonder if I could check out that supposedly incredible picture of you," she said. "The one Elton Keel, that uniquely gifted person, drew in pen."

"Don't make fun," I said, chomping down on my words.

Chelsea's voice rose against the swell of the lunchroom sounds. "I'm just saying it like it is," she said, reminding me of my "lecture" on the bus yesterday.

I took a sip of soda. Chelsea had no right to throw things back in my face like this. But I decided not to make a big deal of it and kept eating.

Chelsea persisted. "What do ya think? Does Elton still have that sketch he did of you?"

"He might," I said. "He carries his artwork around with him everywhere."

Chelsea laughed. "In that plaid little-boy backpack of his?"

Lissa intervened, changing the subject. "I saw him yesterday on Hunsecker Road at the covered bridge," she said. "Looked like he was sketching it."

Was Elton drawing the same thing I was? Too weird.

"There's an old millhouse near that bridge, built back in the 1700's, I think. Maybe that's what he's sketching."

Chelsea grinned. "Bridges, millhouses, and silly girls," she teased. "What an amazing portfolio."

I kept quiet. Chelsea was really pushing things and it bugged me.

Someone yelled my name. "Hey, Merry!"

I turned to see Cody Gower sauntering around with a trayful of food. His usual entourage of male trouble followed.

"Where's the new man in your life?" He shot a grin toward Elton's table.

"Pick on someone else," I said as he passed within punching distance.

"Hey, whatever the retard lover says." He hurled his words back at me as he and his friends spread out, taking up the entire table across from us.

"Hey, dork brain," Chelsea blurted out. "Get a life."

I pushed my tray back. "Oh, so now you're on *my* side."

Chelsea ignored my comment, staring at Cody. "What a total jerk."

Suddenly, Cody's table shook with fierce pounding. The noise caught the attention of everyone in the room. Cody leaped out of his seat. Then he blasted, "This is for *yo-o-ou*, Elton Ke-e-e-el. One, two, three, hit it!"

On cue, the guys at his table—Cody included—began clicking their ball-point pens, held high for everyone to see. The cafeteria rocked with laughter. And my brain nearly exploded.

Elton watched the commotion with a deadpan expression. Who could tell what strange perceptions flitted around inside his childlike mind?

I wanted to get up and give Cody and his cohorts a piece of my insanity. That's when Jon Klein showed up at our table.

Chelsea excused herself almost immediately while Lissa and I filled Jon in on what he'd missed. "It was truly horrible," I said, describing the humiliating act.

Lissa nodded.

"We should do something," I said.

"Like what?" Lissa responded.

"Let's pour soda down Cody's back." I leaped out of my seat ready for justice.

"No, Merry!" Jon grabbed my arm. "That won't solve anything."

I knew he was right. I slumped down in my seat, simmering. "Say that with all *t*'s," I muttered.

Jon grinned. "C'mon, Mer. Let's help Elton instead."

"How?"

Jon picked up his fork. "What about—"

"I know!" I surprised myself with a sudden outburst. "Why don't you invite Elton to our youth service? Remember, we're having that young artist-evangelist from Vermont tomorrow night?"

"Sounds cool enough," Jon said.

"Yeah, he does really great chalk drawings," I said. And since Elton understood the language of pictures . . .

It was pure genius!

The chaos at the next table began to die down. Even though Cody was trying desperately to worm some sort of response out of me, I deliberately refused to react.

Sigh. What if I acted upon everything in my heart? What if everyone did? The world would grind to a horrible end.

"Please, pardon me, pals," Jon said, getting up. He proceeded to walk right up to the table where Elton was still eating . . . and clicking his pen.

Lissa smiled at me, her blue eyes shining. "You really like Jon, don't you?"

"What?"

"Don't ask what, Merry. You know what."

I looked away from her curious smile. "Jon's a good guy."

"And?"

"And we're good friends."

"But?"

"But nothing—that's it." I watched Elton nod his head again and again. "Good! Looks like he wants to come."

"Really?" Lissa turned around to check it out.

I happened to look over at Cody's table just then. It wasn't the sound of pounding or poking fun that made me look. It was the nodding motion of their heads. All of them.

"I hate this," I muttered. "Cody Gower has no heart." I pointed to the rowdy ringleader and his table of followers imitating Elton.

Lissa shook her head. "Guess we oughta invite Cody to the youth meeting, too," she said innocently.

"What?" I said, horrified.

"You know," Lissa said, "seems like Cody could use a good dose of church, or something."

"Something is right," I said under my breath.

I have to admit I wasn't thinking in terms of God or church at that moment. My thoughts were on the seat portion of Cody's blue jeans—as in a powerful, swift kick!

FIVE

By last period, everyone in school had heard the news. Elton Keel had been caught starting a fire in a trash can outside the school. Suspended for three days!

Chelsea, Lissa, and I closed in around Jon's locker, eager for more news. Since Jon worked in the office during last hour, he was the logical person to interrogate.

"Did Elton really do it?" I asked.

"Yeah, did you hear anything?" Lissa probed.

"All I know is I saw Elton come into the principal's office for questioning today."

"When did the fire happen?" I asked.

"Yesterday," Jon said. "Sometime before lunch."

"Did the cops show up?" Lissa's eyes grew wide. "Was my dad one of them?"

"Your dad and his partner were there all right. It was some sad scene," Jon replied. "And Elton confessed to the charge. Well, he never really said he did it—just kept nodding."

Chelsea flung her schoolbag over her shoulder. "C'mon, guys, we've got a bus to catch," she said, dashing for her locker.

Cody Gower and his friends passed us in the hall. "Hey, Merry, what do ya say? Looks like you've got yourself a real live firebug!" he taunted.

Jon spun around. Anger shot from his eyes. "Gower!" he yelled. "Leave Merry out of this."

Cody laughed and elbowed his friends, slinking down the hallway.

I felt sick about Elton. This *had* to be some kind of mistake!

❧   ❧

I wasn't much good for either Lissa or Chelsea on the bus ride home. I played with my camera case, snapping and unsnapping it, reliving my encounter with Elton the previous day.

Mom had a ton of chores lined up for me when I got home. "If you hurry, you'll be done before supper."

"But it's Friday," I whined as she waved her list in my face.

"It's also a very messy Friday," she said with a frown.

Mom was right. My room was messy. I just didn't feel like doing anything about it. Not today.

I curled up on the bed with my wonderful cats—two golden-haired ones and a sleek black one. "Can you say Jon-a-than?" I asked Abednego, my favorite. He seemed more interested in licking his dark coat clean than hearing me moon over some boy.

I couldn't get Jonathan out of my mind. He had, after all, stuck up for me—to Cody Gower of all people.

At times like this, I wished Faithie, my twin sister, were still alive. She wouldn't have minded listening to my triumphs. Or to my tragedies. I thought of Jon's words. *"Leave Merry out of this."* I thought of poor Elton. Playing with fire? Suspended?

I squirmed away from my cats' cozy nest on my bed and went to my dresser. Picking up a gold-framed picture, I stared into the past. Past the world of guys and school. Before the days of curling irons and mousse. To the first real tragedy of my life.

Sitting cross-legged on the rug beside my bed, I cradled the picture in my arms. . . . We were seven then. Our last birthday together . . .

I stared at the picture, remembering the dazzling white pony. Faithie sat behind me in the peppermint-striped saddle, wearing a pink lace dress like mine. She had slipped her arms around my waist, holding on for dear life until the photographer finally succeeded in getting her to smile.

Posing for pictures at that age gets awfully tiresome. But now, as I held the enchanting picture in my arms, I was glad. Glad for all the special times we'd had together. And for the many "firsts" we'd shared. We'd been inseparable friends, Faithie and I. Until the cancer came and took her away.

Mom wandered into my room, and by the look on her face, I knew she wasn't exactly thrilled. "Merry, your room still looks—"

I glanced up. "Oh . . . I'm sorry."

She spied the picture in my arms. "Honey . . . are you all right?" She came and knelt beside me on the floor.

I nodded, tears falling fast.

She swept the hair off my brow, pulling me gently

against her. "Oh, Merry, why didn't you say you needed some space?"

"Please, Mom. I'm okay, really." It felt strange hearing her go on like this.

"You know, Mer, this room has looked a hundred percent worse many, many times before this," she jabbered. "It can certainly look like this for one more day."

"I'll clean it up."

"No, no. It's not necessary, pumpkin. Not today. You just go outside and have a nice long bike ride or do whatever you'd like for a while."

I sat up and looked at her. Smile lines sat on each corner of her mouth; worry lines furrowed her brow. There was a teeny touch of gray every so often in her hair. But love shone out of her deep-set brown eyes. "Thanks for understanding, Mom."

"Any old time." She laughed as she pulled herself up off the floor.

When she was gone, I returned the picture to my dresser. Stepping back, I glimpsed myself in the mirror. How much I had changed!

Merry, the little girl, had disappeared. And in her place stood a young woman. I stared long and hard. How had my twin's death changed me? How had it changed the entire course of my life?

I leaned closer, shifting my gaze to the picture and focusing on Faithie's arms wrapped around me. It seemed I'd always been the strong one. Especially with Faithie. And now even more so with some of my closest friends.

At that moment, I thought of Elton. It startled me that I should think of him in terms of friendship. I felt truly sorry for him. Pure and simple.

Reaching for my backpack, I stuffed my Polaroid camera, sketch pad, and several charcoal pencils inside. Mom was absolutely right. I needed some space, and a long bike ride to Hunsecker's Mill Bridge was just the thing. Quickly, I changed into my grungiest pair of jeans.

I flew down SummerHill Lane on my bike, past the willow grove where Faithie and I had played. Once we hid buried treasures there. Mom wasn't too wild about discovering part of that treasure included the wedding band she had innocently removed while washing dishes. After a whole day of digging, I retrieved it in time to avoid major disciplinary action.

Farther down the lane, Zooks' farm was hopping with Amish folk. Looked like a quilting bee. I scanned the women milling around on the front porch, probably having a lemonade break—the real stuff, freshly squeezed, of course. I looked for Rachel, but didn't see her.

In the field beyond the Zook farmhouse, Levi and Aaron were tilling the soil, preparing for corn planting. With a little help from their mules.

Soon, the cemetery came into view. We'd buried Faithie there nearly seven years ago. A warm breeze rippled through my hair as I stood up, pedaling hard. Standing on tiptoes, I could see the top of her gravestone peeking over a small rise in the graveyard. A feeling of uncontrollable joy filled me as I flew down the lane. Faithie's soul, her true self, wasn't stuck away in that old grave. She was alive. And someday in heaven I would see her again.

The joyful feeling turned to one of quiet resolve and

I sat down on the seat of my bike, letting my legs rest as I coasted toward Hunsecker Road.

At the intersection, I looked both ways before heading down the road to the covered bridge. As I made the last turn before the bridge, I heard the loose boards clatter under the weight of a car as it drove across the one-laner. The sound lingered in my mind until the car honked and I saw Miss Spindler, our neighbor, waving. I waved back, wondering what Old Hawk Eyes was doing out here. Probably spying—her favorite hobby.

She turned the corner in her snazzy red car, grinding the clutch as usual. I waited till she was gone before parking my bike on the narrow shoulder near the bridge. Then I ran through the high grass along the bank of the Conestoga River.

Finding just the right vantage point, I sat under two large oaks that leaned together overhead, as though locking arms in friendship. I took two shots of the bridge with my Polaroid, then sat down and began to sketch while the pictures developed.

Insects buzzed around me. Martins swept down to the river's edge, searching for a worm supper as the cool, sweet smell of April filled my senses. Taking all the time in the world, I referred back to the Polaroid pictures, now very clear. Sometimes photographs called attention to things missed in real life.

I put the finishing touches on my sketch, confident that Mrs. Hawkins would be truly pleased with the finished project.

The sound of a horse and buggy caught my attention. When I looked up, I saw an Amish couple in an open courting buggy make the sharp turn just before heading into the covered bridge. Rachel had said covered bridges were made for kissing. Maybe a kiss was on the way. . . .

I had the strongest urge to sneak up on the couple, and I probably would have if I hadn't noticed a blond-haired boy sitting high in the twin oaks above me. Squinting up into the afternoon sun, I shielded my eyes, calling to him. "Elton, is that you?"

He nodded again and again.

"What are you doing up there?"

He held his sketch pad high, his eyes shining.

"That's good." I felt awkward. I wanted to ask why he'd taken my idea and sketched this bridge, but the more I thought of it, the more I decided it was a compliment, not a threat. "Are you okay up there?"

He nodded repeatedly.

"How far along is your sketch?"

Without warning, Elton scrambled down from the tree. He leaned over to show off his drawing.

"Wow! It's genius!" I raved, still sitting on the grassy bank. How could a sensitive kid like Elton draw a picture like this, start a fire, and get suspended all in one week?

Elton stood there with a haunting, hollow-eyed look on his face. Was he waiting for me to show *my* drawing of the bridge? More awkward seconds passed.

"Oh no, you don't," I said, laughing, realizing I was right about what Elton wanted. "My sketch needs major help compared to yours."

I stood up, noticing a bike parked beside mine near the bridge. Probably his. Brushing off my jeans, I loaded my backpack. "Here, pick one," I said, holding up the Polaroid pictures.

He studied them carefully before choosing. Then he nodded.

"Oh, it's nothing. I take pictures here all the time. Everywhere, really," I said more to myself than to him. And with camera in hand, I headed up the riverbank. "I have to leave now."

Elton stared almost sadly as I waved goodbye. I wondered how on earth he'd arrived here without me noticing.

By the time I reached my bike, the Amish buggy was emerging very slowly from the bridge. I grinned at the couple as they rode out. Time for more than one kiss, I thought, as the horse picked up speed and pranced down the road.

SIX

Saturday morning, bright and early . . . well, really more like around nine-thirty, I got up and tore into my messy room. The cleaning lady was coming in a couple days, but Mom always liked the house picked up for the occasion. I never could figure out why we had to scour the house for the cleaning lady's arrival. Seemed like a waste of money. And energy.

After brunch I headed to Rachel's. She wanted to make a patchwork pillow for my hope chest and said I should choose the colors. When I arrived, she was helping her mother bake bread for tomorrow's noon meal. It was the Zooks' turn to have church at their house, and since the Amish always shared a meal after the service, it was essential that food preparations were completed before sundown Saturday.

"What are you serving tomorrow?" I peered over Rachel's shoulder.

"The usual," she said, showing me cold cuts, red beets, pickles, and cheese already cooling in the refrigerator run on 12-volt batteries.

Rachel's face grew serious. "Something else happened yesterday." She motioned me to the corner of the kitchen, out of her mother's hearing range. "Our chickens all died," she said quietly. "Someone poisoned them."

"That's horrible!"

I must've spoken too loudly because Rachel's mother looked startled as she set two loaves of bread out to cool on the sideboard. "*Ach*, Rachel! Hold your tongue."

That was the end of that. Rachel clammed right up, obeying her mother. Even after she took me to her bedroom to choose squares of various colors for my pillow, she refused to discuss it.

I did not like this Ben Fisher person. Anyone who could kill off innocent chickens—it was the most hideous thing I'd ever heard. Big Bad Ben was inching closer and closer to the Zook family. What would he do next?

On the way home I was so deep in thought, fussing and fuming about Ben Fisher, I nearly walked right over Elton Keel sitting in the thickest part of the willow grove.

Willow branches draped around us, forming a canopy so dense that the sun only filtered through it, casting whispers of light here and there. It was a *very* secret place.

"Elton, what are you doing here?"

He pulled his legs up next to his chest and rested his chin on his knees, squinting up at me. That's when I saw his plaid backpack and the sketch pad lying on the grass beside him.

"Oh, you're sketching again."

He started nodding.

"May I see?"

Elton reached for his sketch pad. He pointed to the

Zooks' barn in the distance and then to his pad. The drawing was an exact replica of the huge white barn, complete with silo. I stared in awe at the pen sketch. Flawless artistry.

"Oo-oh, Elton. This is so-o good."

He clicked his pen without stopping. The clicking seemed to provide a sense of security.

Suddenly, I had a great idea. "Want to borrow my Polaroid for a while? You can sketch from the photos at home. Sometimes it helps catch details you might've missed."

Elton didn't move his head, but his eyes said yes.

"Are you coming to the youth service?" I closed the sketch pad and handed it back to him.

He stopped clicking his pen and began to nod.

"I'll bring the camera tonight, okay?"

His nodding continued.

I was dying to ask him about the fire at school. Why he'd started it. What had really happened. But almost before I finished thinking that thought, Elton turned abruptly and reached for his backpack.

"Are you leaving?" I asked.

His attention seemed focused on whatever he was searching for in his backpack. Then slowly, and with a high-pitched grunt, he pulled out a folded paper. Its edges were charred black and flaking off. Elton handed the paper to me.

I took the fragile paper from his hand. "Is this for me?"

He nodded. Only once.

His reaction startled me. In the short time I'd known

Elton, he'd never ever nodded only once.

Carefully, I unfolded the charred paper. My breath caught in my throat as I recognized the sketch. It was the drawing of me—the one Elton had given; the one I'd returned.

I squinted at the fair-faced boy. With a totally blank look, Elton stared back. It occurred to me that if I observed him long enough, carefully enough, I might find my answers in his eyes.

A sudden breeze made the willows whisper above us and the drawing tremble in my hand. Between alternating intervals of shade and sun, flickers of light played on Elton's face. "You want to tell me something, don't you?"

He nodded one time.

"Do you want to tell me why you started the fire at school?"

Again, he nodded. More quickly.

"Okay," I said. "Here's what we'll do. I ask the questions and you give the answers. One nod means yes, and nothing means no. Okay?"

He nodded. This was incredible!

"Did you start the fire by burning my picture—this picture?" I held up the charred drawing, tapping it lightly.

He nodded.

"Were you mad at Cody Gower?"

Not a single eyelash fluttered.

"Were you mad at the others who teased you?"

Nothing.

"Were you—" I paused. What other reason could there be?

Elton waited for me to finish, his blond hair dazzling

white, halolike, as the sun danced on it.

I inspected the sketch again. The "4 U" jumped out at me. Then I remembered Chelsea's comment yesterday. *"He's probably depressed."* That's exactly what she'd said! Elton would be depressed if I gave the sketch back. Maybe, for once, Chelsea was right.

I held up the drawing, charred edges and all. "Were you upset because I didn't keep this?"

He paused almost thoughtfully, then began nodding.

I felt lousy about the part I'd played in his wanting to burn the picture. "I'm really sorry if I upset you, Elton. I only wanted you to get a good grade," I explained. "Well, I better get going. I have homework to do before youth service."

Elton picked up his sketch pad and began to draw as I headed down the narrow dirt path toward the road. I called, waving the charred picture in my hand, "Goodbye—and thanks." But Elton was already preoccupied with his work.

I kicked at the stones along the side of the road. Bottom line: I was partly responsible for the trash-can fire. Elton had been offended by my returning his sketch. And I was sorry.

Almost home, I heard a buggy speeding down the lane behind me. I knew it was Levi Zook just by the way he handled his spirited horse. Everyone knew he was a hotroddin' buggy driver. He yanked on the reins as I turned around, pulling the buggy off the road.

"It's a good thing they don't let you drive a car," I teased, hiding Elton's drawing behind my back.

Levi stood up in his open buggy, tipping his wide-brimmed straw hat. "Going my way?"

"Better watch it, Levi. You don't want the bishops to find out, do you?"

He grinned. "Find out what? That you're goin' riding with me?"

I shrugged my shoulders, feeling the warmth creep into my face. "Says who?"

"*You* could say it if you wanted to, Merry Hanson." Levi was flirting like crazy. It was a good thing he was in his *Rumschpringa,* the Amish term for the running-around years before baptism into the church. Amish teens were allowed to experience the outside world and decide whether or not to return to their roots. Most of them did.

Levi put his foot up on the rim of the buggy and leaned on his leg. He was still smiling. "How about to-night? Jah?"

"I'm sorry, Levi. I don't think it's such a good idea."

He flashed a smile. "Why not?"

I looked down at my feet. Why was my heart beating like this?

"Merry?" His voice was mellow and sweet. And gently persistent.

Without looking up, I found myself saying something like, "Well, maybe . . . sometime."

You would've thought he'd gotten a yes on a marriage proposal, because in a split second, Levi sat down, slapped the reins across his beautiful Belgian horse, and took off.

The wild way he drove that buggy called for a good nickname. That's when I thought of Zap 'em Zook.

Wouldn't the Alliteration Wizard be proud?

SEVEN

When I arrived home, I called Lissa to invite her to spend the night. She agreed to bring her things to youth service and ride home with Skip and me afterward.

"Thanks for asking," she said on the phone, "besides, I really need to talk to you."

"About what?"

"Something personal."

I felt nervous. "Is everything still okay at home?"

"I'm fine, Merry. It's not that."

"Then what?"

"It's nothing to worry about. It's just—" She stopped.

"What?"

Lissa hesitated before saying softly, "Okay, it's about Jon Klein and—"

Skip yelled, "Supper!" in my ear.

I covered the receiver, glaring at him. "Can't you see I'm on the phone?"

He shrugged uncaringly. "Mom said to get yourself to the table fast; we're running late."

I tried to shoo him away, but he kept hanging around, acting like a real dope. Finally, I turned back to the phone. "Sorry, Liss. Guess we'll just have to talk later, when we can talk in *private*," I said loudly for Skip's benefit.

Lissa said goodbye and we hung up. I raced Skip to the kitchen, wondering what sort of personal thing Lissa had to tell me about Jon.

Later, when Skip and I showed up at church, it was crowded. I spotted Jon and Elton in the lobby. Jon looked wonderful as always, tall and with an air of confidence. Elton seemed nervous, though. His eyes darted back and forth, and I wondered if he'd ever been inside a church building before.

Since two other local youth groups had joined us for the service, seating was limited. I hurried to claim the empty chair beside Lissa, placing my Polaroid camera under my seat. If we'd arrived sooner, I might've asked her what was so important about Jon, right then and there.

Soon Jon, with Elton following close behind, found seats at the far end of our row. Jon leaned over and smiled at us, but Elton sat straight and rigid, staring at the platform where the musicians were warming up. I decided to wait till later to hand over my camera.

After the second praise chorus, Lissa whispered, "Do you think Elton's into this at all?"

"You might be surprised."

There were the usual announcements about social events going on during April, but I was most interested in the upcoming Spinster's Spree, two weeks from today. It was an annual thing at our church. Girls could invite the boy of their choice to the church-sponsored dinner.

We were also expected to pay for his meal and the after-dinner entertainment.

Was it possible that what Lissa wanted to tell me about Jon had something to do with the Spinster's Spree? Maybe she'd heard that Jon wanted me to ask him! *That* kind of talk would be sweet music to my ears.

I hadn't gone last year, mainly because I was too shy to ask anyone. This year, however, I hoped to get up the nerve.

While the youth pastor plugged the spree, Lissa looked at me curiously. "You going?"

I shrugged. No sense telling her till I knew if Jon agreed.

After several songs, the offering, and a couple numbers by a local Christian band, the special speaker was introduced. "I am happy to have a very talented artist, Anthony Fritchey, with us tonight . . . all the way from Vermont." The youth pastor grinned and sat down.

Everyone clapped, welcoming Anthony to our church.

A tripod with a green chalkboard stood ready. Anthony picked up a piece of chalk and quickly drew a giant ant, then made a plus sign. Next to that, a two-thousand weight, another plus sign, and a quick sketch of a human knee. "What's my name?" he called, pointing to each of the three symbols.

"Ant-ton-knee," we all shouted. The service was off to a great start. I crossed my legs and settled back in my seat, eager to watch the work of this artist-evangelist. I'd heard of people using their talents for the Lord, but I'd never seen an artist do chalk drawings to inspirational music.

Beginning with a choral piece, "God So Loved the World," as a backdrop, Anthony created a detailed sketch before our eyes. His hand movements were quick, yet graceful, as he portrayed God saying goodbye to His only Son as Jesus prepared to leave heaven.

Deftly, Anthony drew one scene after another, telling the story of Jesus' short life on planet earth. When it came time for the picture of Jesus hanging on the cross, most of the kids were leaning forward on their seats, spellbound. It was so moving the way Anthony portrayed the pain, the agony, in Jesus' face.

God's Son was dying for us!

I happened to look over at Elton. To my surprise, big tears rolled unchecked down his face. Forcing my gaze away from him, I prayed silently, tears coming to my own eyes as I tried to focus my attention on the grand resurrection scene coming up. The "Hallelujah Chorus" set the stage for the triumphal moment, and I wanted to cheer as the artist finished his incredible work.

Unprepared for Elton's initial reaction, I was even more surprised when he stood up and began clapping slowly and somewhat awkwardly. In a moment, all of us were on our feet applauding, not so much for the unique evangelist, but for the realization of truth he'd just created.

My heart was warmed by Elton's response. Was this the first time he'd heard the gospel? I honestly didn't know. Anyway, lots of kids greeted Elton after the service, encouraging him to come back.

Lissa and I went over to say hi. When I gave Elton my camera and showed him how to use it, I watched his eyes. Even though his face was expressionless, I was sure I saw the beginnings of a twinkle in his eyes. The windows to his soul.

❧   ❧

Lissa got started talking about Elton on the way home. Skip didn't act a bit interested. He was too "cool." Some older brothers were like that.

"Why'd you give him your camera?" Lissa asked.

"It's a good way to record the things you're sketching," I explained in spite of Skip's rude looks. "I use it all the time."

"Aren't you afraid he'll lose it or something?" she asked.

"Not if it's in his backpack. He wears it everywhere."

Lissa was silent for a moment. Then she asked, "What do you think is wrong with Elton?"

"I think he's lots smarter than people give him credit for," I said, turning around to face Lissa in the backseat. I didn't tell her about the "conversation" I'd had with Elton in the willow grove earlier. Skip would never let me live it down. I was surprised he hadn't overreacted about the camera by now.

"Does anyone know why he can't talk?" she asked.

Skip turned on the radio. "Ever hear of autism?" he said, as if he knew what he was talking about. "Maybe that's his problem."

"It seems as if he's always daydreaming," Lissa said. "Do you think he's out of touch with reality?"

"No!" I said, surprised at my outburst.

Skip gave me a sideways look. "My little Merry sounds pretty sure of herself tonight," he taunted.

"Don't call me your little anything," I said.

"Yeah, yeah," Skip muttered, turning up the volume on the radio. "Bet you'll be mighty ticked when he wrecks your precious Polaroid." There. Skip hadn't disappointed me after all.

I turned around, looking at Lissa again. "See what you're missing out on by being an only child?"

Lissa gave me a half smile. Her biggest wish was to have a sister or brother. She'd often said how lonely it was being the only kid in a house where both parents worked. At least now her father was sober. And going to therapy every week.

Skip checked both ways before turning off Hunsecker Road. One thing for sure, my brother was a careful driver. Nothing like Zap 'em Zook.

We passed acres of pastureland and Amish farmhouses. I stared as we came up on the Fishers' place. Was Ben at home or out causing more trouble?

Skip looked at me. "Sounds like Ben Fisher really had a run-in with the Amish bishops."

"I heard about it."

"He's only got two weeks before his probation's up and they kick him out of the Amish church," Skip said.

Then unexpectedly, just ahead, something blocked the road. "Watch out!" I shouted.

Skip slammed on the brakes. Our brights were shining on a herd of . . .

"Cows! Abe Zook's milk cows are out!" Skip hollered, leaping out of the car.

I unsnapped my seat belt and hopped out with Skip. "How on earth did they get loose?"

"One guess," Skip said sarcastically. I knew he was thinking of Ben Fisher. "You better run and alert the Zooks." He got in the car and backed it up slowly, turning off the headlights.

"Looks like everyone's in bed already," I said, motioning for Lissa to come with me.

Skip turned off the ignition. "They'll be glad you got them up. Hurry, Mer." And he headed off to start rounding up the cattle.

My heart pounded ninety miles an hour as Lissa and I hurried up the Zooks' lane. Twenty-four dairy cows roaming loose was nothing to sneeze at. Those cows were the lifeblood of our neighbor's income. With every step, I became more furious with Ben Fisher. Or whoever had done this horrible thing.

EIGHT

It was almost midnight by the time we got the cows in the barn. Levi volunteered to sleep outside to keep watch. It struck me as very noble. Noble and loyal. My thoughts spun a web of admiration for my longtime friend, Levi Zap 'em Zook.

The second oldest son of Abe Zook was, and always had been, a friend to the end. Flirtatious, true, but when it came right down to it, there was no way on this wide earth I'd ever be hearing about Levi being hauled off to the Amish bishop!

Abe thanked us for our help and offered to give us money as we left.

"We've been your neighbors all these years," Skip said, waving his hand. "No need to start acting like strangers now."

Abe slapped Skip on the back, grinning. Skip was right, of course. And for the first time in ages, I felt proud to be called his little Merry.

Once we got home, Lissa and I were wiped out. Too exhausted to have our private talk. Whatever she had to say about Jon Klein would have to wait till morning.

❧ ❧

The familiar sound of clip-clopping seemed to come and go as it mingled with my early morning dreams. Had it not been Sunday, I would've been content simply to sleep away the exhaustion of the night before. But Sundays were the Lord's day at our house, and no matter how late we'd gotten to bed the night before, Sunday mornings meant early rising.

It wasn't just difficult to wake up Lissa, it was next to impossible. She had burrowed herself into my blue-striped comforter. I piled my sleepy cat trio, Shadrach, Meshach, and Abednego, on top of her. A moan drifted out of the blankets. Abednego took it as a signal to play. He pawed at the covers, leaping on the mound that was Lissa's head.

"Rise and shine!" Dad's deep voice resonated through the hallway.

"Lissa," I said, shaking her. "Better wake up, or we won't have time to talk."

While I waited for her to respond, I stared at my collection of framed photography on the far wall—my gallery. It was a display area for my best work. Everything from scenes of trees in autumn and Amish windmills to Faithie's gravestone adorned the wall.

"C'mon, Lissa. Wake up!" I jostled her some more.

"I'm tired," came her sleepy voice. "Can't you shower first?"

"Only if you promise you'll be up when I'm finished."

She giggled under the covers. "You sound like a drill sergeant."

"Well I am, and you'd better get up or—"

"Merry," Mom called through the door. "I need you downstairs as soon as possible."

"Okay," I said, feeling cheated. Now when would I get to hear what Lissa had on her mind?

On my way to the closet, I passed my bulletin board. Elton's charred sketch of me hung in the middle of it. I studied the drawing for a moment, once again amazed at his talent.

By the time I was out of the shower, Lissa was dancing around, anxious to claim some privacy in the bathroom. Quickly, I dressed and towel dried my hair in my room, waiting for her to come back out and get her clothes before her shower. But she was taking forever and soon Mom was calling again. Frustrated, I left my room and hurried downstairs.

"Looks as if the Zooks are having church today," Dad said as he stood at the sink gazing out the window. "Good thing they got those milk cows back in the barn last night."

"Sure would like to know who'd do such a thing," I said, setting the table. "Cows don't get out by themselves, you know."

He turned around, wearing a serious look on his unshaven face. "I think it's time the police heard about Ben Fisher, don't you, hon?"

Mom grabbed the skillet out of the pantry. "It's hard to know what to say or do," she said, pouring a cup of pancake mix into a bowl. "The Amish have their own way of dealing with things like this."

I spoke up. "But Dad's right. Something should be

done, before someone gets hurt." I hesitated to say more. Rachel would be upset if I told my parents everything that had been happening.

Dad kept talking. The more he talked, the more I realized he already knew about everything. The hate mail, the broken window, the poisoned chickens . . . everything.

"I think I'll go over and have a neighborly chat with Abe," Dad said, stroking his prickly chin.

Since the Amish Sunday meeting usually meant sitting around and visiting long after the noon meal, Abe Zook would be busy with his friends and relatives till afternoon milking. I reminded Dad of that.

"That's true," he said. "And we'll be getting home too late from our evening service for me to go over then." The Amish always went to bed with the chickens, around nine or so—whether they had any or not.

"Should I tell Rachel you're coming tomorrow?" I asked.

Mom spun around, her hand steadying the mixing bowl. "That's not such a good idea," she said. "I don't want you getting involved with this, Merry. It sounds a bit dangerous to me."

"But Rachel's my friend!"

She nodded. "The Zooks are good neighbors and fine people, but they don't meddle in our affairs." She sighed, casting a look which I interpreted to be a plea for unity. From Dad. "My vote is we let them work things out according to their traditions."

Dad pulled out a chair and sat down, opening the Bible and leaning it against his empty plate. His eyebrows danced as he turned a deaf ear to Mom's chatter. Dad, being a medical doctor, focused his life on helping people. That's probably where I got my strong inclination to do the same.

Anyway, out of nowhere, Elton Keel popped into my mind. Maybe it was because he was always silent. Dad, on the other hand, was only trying to be silent at the moment. I resolved with more determination than ever to help Elton fit into our school, and possibly our church.

Lissa showed up for devotions at the same time Skip did. My brother appeared dressed and ready to walk out the door for church, but Lissa still wore her bathrobe. I could tell by his sideways glance that he thought Lissa was totally uncool coming that way to breakfast.

Maybe he'd forgotten Lissa's background. Her father had an abusive streak and nearly every time he got drunk, Lissa and her mom had suffered beatings. The cycle of abuse had gone on most of her life, until last November when Mr. Vyner turned himself in and started getting help. Lissa told me once she couldn't remember ever sitting down with her parents and sharing a family breakfast. Maybe that's why she liked it here so much.

As Dad read the morning devotional, I wished there was something I could do to get Skip to be polite to my friend. I thought of kicking him under the table, but that seemed a bit childish. Besides, I was sure Skip had only one thing on his mind at the moment. Food!

After a breakfast of pancakes and scrambled eggs, I hurried around the kitchen, assisting Mom by clearing the table and loading the dishwasher. Lissa excused herself and went upstairs to dress. Skip stuck his head in the refrigerator, searching for more food.

Mom ignored the Bottomless Pit. "Thanks for your help, Merry," she said as I finished up.

"Any time." I dried my hands on her strawberry towel. Mom had no idea why I was hurrying around. The truth was if I finished up fast in the kitchen, Lissa and I would have time for our talk. But I was wrong.

Halfway up the back stairs, I heard someone pounding at the kitchen door. I waited, listening, as Skip flew past me with two pieces of jelly bread. "You're gonna be late, cat breath," he said.

"Go away," I muttered, listening for some clues from the kitchen.

Soon Mom called, "Merry, it's Rachel."

My throat went dry. What on earth was Rachel Zook doing here with church going on at her house?

I sensed trouble. Big trouble.

NINE

Rachel was waiting for me in the kitchen wearing a Sunday dress of bright purple and a black apron.

I greeted her. "Hi, Rachel. You okay?"

She nodded, but I knew better. Rachel wasn't her cheery self. When kids grow up together, it's easy to know things like that.

Mom left the room to get ready, and probably to give us some privacy. When she was out of sight, Rachel spoke softly. "Can you come over this afternoon?"

"What's up?"

She touched the strings on her *kapp*—the white prayer bonnet—on her head. "There's a culprit that needs to be caught," she whispered.

I didn't have to be told what she was referring to. Evidently, the Zooks wanted proof that Ben Fisher was the one causing trouble for them.

"So your parents want me to help, is that it?" I asked, a little surprised.

Rachel shook her head. "No, no. Mam and Dat don't know a thing about this and we must keep it that way. My brother and I want you to help us do a little spying." She

65

took a deep breath. "To help our family."

"Levi and you?"

She nodded. "I'll tell you later when you come what we've got planned. Jah?"

I walked with her to the door. "Are you saying you're taking things into your own hands?"

Her eyes brightened. "You may call it what you wish, dear cousin." Rachel liked to call me cousin, even though we were only distant ones. Our family trees branched back to the same Anabaptist ancestors. She gave me a long hug, then hurried out the door and down the steps.

I waved as she passed the white gazebo in our back-yard. "You can always count on me," I called. Grinning, Rachel returned my wave.

I closed the back door and made some tracks of my own. When Dad wanted to walk out the door on Sundays, the family had better be ready. It was the one day of the week he showed little patience for stragglers.

Thanks to Lissa, my new curling iron was fired up and ready to go. Briskly, I brushed my hair, wondering about Lissa. Had it been my imagination, or was she avoiding me today?

Quickly, I applied some makeup, leaning close to the mirror as I brushed on some blush and a smidgen of lip-stick. Actually, Mom didn't care how much makeup I used, as long as it was in good taste. Her approach made me feel sorry for some of the church girls my age. They weren't allowed to wear much of anything on their faces.

I skipped the mascara. Instead, I spent the last few minutes fluffing my hair; all the while a nagging thought threatened my peace of mind. Had Lissa changed her mind about having our personal talk? She'd gone downstairs to call her mom about something. Was it a stall tactic?

I was snatching up my purse and camera, and saying goodbye to my cats, when Lissa burst into the room. "I can't hold it in any longer, Merry."

I stared at her. "Hold what in?"

"Do you like Jon Klein or not?"

I looked at my bulletin board and Elton's burnt drawing, avoiding her stare. "How many times do you have to ask?" I said.

"Well, do you?"

"He's just a friend." I didn't even say a good friend. I didn't want anyone to know how I really felt about the Alliteration Wizard. It wasn't like Lissa was my best friend or anything. In fact, I didn't really have a best friend anymore. Not since Faithie died.

Slowly, I turned around. Lissa sat on the edge of my bed, looking up at me like she had something earthshaking to say.

I inched toward her. "What is it, Liss?"

Quickly, she looked down, playing with her tiny gold bracelet. "I guess you could say . . . I kinda like Jon."

My heart stopped. "You mean you like Jon, uh, as in boyfriend?"

She nodded, her blue eyes wistful. "I think I sorta do, Merry. I mean . . . oh, I don't know if I can do this."

"Do what?" I could tell she was having a whammy of a time.

"I really wanted to have this talk with you."

"So, what's the point? We're talking, aren't we?"

She sighed. "Well, that Spinster's Spree thing is next weekend, and I just thought . . ." She stopped.

I wanted her to speed it up, spit it out.

Her eyes shone. "I think I want to ask Jon to be my date next Saturday." She stood up quickly, like she'd said something she was sorry for. "Oh, Merry, you're not mad, are you?"

My heart had stopped beating, but I managed to say, "Mad? Why should I be mad?"

She came over and hugged me, blubbering something about being awfully grateful.

Grateful? I probably would've freaked out right in my own bedroom if Dad hadn't called up the stairs just then. And I must admit I don't even remember the ride to church. Frustration had taken on a life of its own. And that was putting it mildly.

We strolled into Sunday school together, Lissa and I. But I felt like a walking prayer request. If someone had taken my up-to-the-minute spiritual temperature, I might've passed for a corpse. Thanks to that private talk with Lissa. Worse yet, I noticed Jon sitting with our new pastor's daughter, the beautiful Ashley Horton.

Lissa leaned over. "When should I ask him?" she whispered.

I toyed with telling her to go over right now, in front of the competition, but being a Christian friend was more important than any sarcastic comment I could've made. Besides, Lissa was one of my converts. I had led her to the Lord four months ago. She certainly didn't need her "older" sister in Christ acting like a jerk.

"Wait till after class," I suggested, as calmly as possible.

Our teacher, Mrs. Simms, arrived dressed in a rose-colored challis shirtdress; her blond hair in its usual free-fall style hung down past her shoulders. I wasn't surprised when she started in by giving us girls a pep talk. "Don't be shy about inviting someone for Spinster's Spree," she said, smiling. "This is your moment, ladies. The opportunity you've been waiting for." She pushed her long hair behind one ear. "And guys, make things easy for the girls, okay? Be sweet."

I happened to notice Jon's face brighten at that remark. Only there was a problem: he was looking at Ashley!

I glanced at Lissa. She'd noticed, too.

Just then, Elton Keel came in dressed in tan dress slacks and a brown short-sleeved shirt. He was wearing his red-and-blue plaid backpack. From where I sat, it looked like my Polaroid might've found a home inside.

Mrs. Simms stopped everything to welcome him to class. He spied me and with a childish wave, headed toward my row of chairs. Lissa and I slid over to make room for him, and although some kids might've felt uneasy sitting next to a special ed. guy with a firebug label, it didn't bother me one bit. I knew the truth.

Seeing him here made my day. Maybe I wasn't such a spiritual zombie after all. I offered to share my Bible, even though it was next to impossible to keep my thoughts focused on Mrs. Simms and the Sunday school lesson. Besides replaying Lissa's conversation with me, I had to endure Jon sitting next to Ashley, probably the prettiest girl in church. Ashley was not only pretty, she was also the epitome of goodness. Which smashed the preachers'-kids-are-rotten theory to pieces. I could only hope that Ashley Horton had no brains. That, and that alone, might give me an edge with the Alliteration Wizard.

In order to take my mind off this truly stressful situation, I tried to decide on my favorite month of the year. Sometimes a mental exercise can mean the difference between surviving and not.

The best month of all was a toss-up between September, my birthday month, and October, the last days before winter's power punch. I loved the sound of October leaves under my feet—like walking on a field of Rice Krispies.

In the midst of my deciding, I observed my friend Lissa. She seemed intent on the lesson. Or was her concentration on Jon?

Elton, on the other hand, seemed content just being here. He held his beloved pen in his left hand without clicking it. I wondered about that. Was it a gauge, a way to determine how attentive he really was?

Silence is golden, my dad always said. But in Elton's case, silence was much more than that. Silence spoke of childlike wonder. A world secluded—inside his head. Elton's world was a place where things like seeing a chalk drawing of Jesus dying on a cross brought shameless tears. A world where discovering an oak tree near a covered bridge and settling down for an afternoon of sketching brought peace.

I was sure I was beginning to know Elton. Really

know him. He was letting me in, allowing me to see inside. In Elton's world, things like the Spinster's Spree and a preacher's daughter with good looks didn't matter. I smiled at him and turned my attention back to the lesson.

Honestly, if Elton hadn't come today, I'd probably have had a nervous breakdown.

TEN

After class, I waited while Lissa went to talk to Jon. I watched her approach him, realizing none of this would be happening if I had asked him weeks ago. Of course, it was anybody's guess what his answer might've been. Maybe if I had asked him with all *w*'s . . .

Elton remained seated next to me. I turned to face him. "Did you like the class?"

He nodded.

"I'm glad you came today."

Again, he nodded.

"Are you staying for church?"

He tapped on my Bible, then pointed to me.

I laughed. "Sure, I'm staying, and you can borrow my Bible if you want to."

He shook his head no.

I was stunned. I didn't know Elton could do that. "Are you saying you don't want to use my Bible?"

He shook his head, emphatically no.

"What then? What do you mean?" I was feeling totally inadequate here.

He pointed to me again. Then, very precisely, he pointed to himself.

"Oh, I get it," I said, relieved. "You want to sit with me in church and share my Bible?"

He nodded and forced a half smile.

I could hardly contain my joy. Elton was changing, growing before my eyes! I explained to him that my parents thought being together as a family in church on Sunday mornings was somehow important to God. "So . . . if you don't mind sitting with all of us, we're set."

Elton nodded and when he did, I saw a hint of a smile in his eyes.

Lissa came over and stood beside me. One glance told me Jon had turned her down.

"Guess who beat me to it." She pointed discreetly to the door.

Elton stayed in the room while Lissa pushed me into the hall. "Ashley's taking Jon to Spinster's Spree," she moaned.

My stomach rumbled. Conflict made me hungry. "Come with me," I said.

"Where are we going?" Lissa asked, following me as I rushed toward the classroom down the hall from ours. The smell of freshly brewed coffee and sweet doughnuts drew me inside. Adults stood around, doing whatever it was they did every Sunday with coffee in hand. My dad spotted me and waved between bites of pastry.

"Here, eat this," I said, handing Lissa a jelly-filled doughnut.

Her eyes grew wide. "What's *your* problem?" She sounded like she was going to cry.

I shrugged, chewing quickly.

"What should I do about Spinster's Spree?"

I had to be careful what I said. After all, she had absolutely no idea how I felt about Jon. Most likely the thing with Ashley Horton was only temporary. Once Jon found out she was basically illiterate, he'd turn back to the Word Woman—me.

Meanwhile, I needed a way to distract Lissa, to get her mind off Jon. "Have you thought of asking someone else?"

"Like who?"

I wiped my mouth. "Hey, it's not the end of the world, is it . . . I mean getting beat out by Ashley Horton?" I was trying to play it down. For her sake, and mine. "There are plenty more guys to pick from."

"Look, maybe you don't know it, but I saw Ashley's Sunday school lesson book," Lissa said, lowering her voice.

"So? What's that got to do with anything?"

"She thinks she's pretty cool—I mean, she's got her initials written all over everywhere. A.H. this, and A.H. that."

I smiled. "Very clever. AH-H-H never would've guessed."

Lissa and I burst out laughing. That's when I realized we were the only ones left in the room.

"Listen," I said, touching Lissa's elbow. "Sounds like the organ music started. We'd better skedaddle."

I wiped the sticky off the corners of my mouth and hurried into the hall. Elton was waiting near the stairs. "Ready for church?" I asked.

He nodded.

"C'mon, Lissa," I said. "By the way, Elton's sitting with us today."

She looked like she hadn't heard me right, but I threatened her with a frown. She kept her mouth shut and followed me up the stairs, behind Elton.

❧   ❧

During the service when people greet each other, I introduced Elton to my parents and my brother. Dad and Mom were ultra polite as usual, but Skip didn't exhibit the kind of enthusiasm I'd hoped for. In fact, he was downright rude. I shouldn't have been surprised. What can you expect from a seventeen-year-old sibling who hates stray cats—stray anything! Right about now, I was sure Skip was thinking about Elton as my latest stray, er . . . project.

When we settled into the pew again, I sent a serious scowl Skip's way.

He pretended not to notice. Then, out of the corner of his mouth came this: "Don't be such a child, Merry."

Fortunately for my obnoxious brother, church services were designed to discourage fighting, whether verbal or a solid punch in the nose. In my opinion, Skip truly deserved the latter.

Anyway, God must've been looking out for me, because the minute our pastor announced his text, I recognized the verse—Matthew 18:3. And Skip, being the snooty high school senior he was, tried to act totally cool when the pastor's word rang out from the pulpit. "I tell you the truth, unless you change and become like little children, you will never enter the kingdom of heaven."

Not only was the verse fair reward for Skip's snide remark, it spoke an even deeper, more powerful message to me. I thought of Elton's childlike ways—often misunderstood by his peers. His simple approach to life was probably a very refreshing change to God. It must be much easier for the Lord to work in an uncomplicated life.

Finding the chapter and verse in my Bible was a snap, but sharing God's Word with Elton like this, holding my end of the Bible while he held his end, seemed almost symbolic. Rachel Zook would probably say it was providential—that God had led Elton to me so that I could lead him to Jesus. She was always talking about things like that. Simply put, it meant she believed that whatever happened to her and her family had been permitted by God. That's why the Zooks wouldn't press charges against Ben Fisher. Even if we caught him.

Rachel and I had discussed it many times, but I still struggled with the whole thing of trusting God one hundred percent, amen. It was especially hard for me since I liked to take care of things myself.

I listened to the pastor talk about the kind of faith a little child exhibits when he or she comes to God. But my mental image of Elton and the tears rolling down his cheeks last night spoke louder than any sermon.

Staring at the floor under the pew in front of me, I noticed Elton's backpack. I'd seen the contents on more than one occasion. Pens, paper, sketch pad, and my Polaroid. Something was missing, though. Elton needed a Bible, and one way or other, I was going to make sure he got one.

When the congregation stood up for the benediction, I noticed Jon Klein sitting with his two older sisters. Quickly, I bowed my head during prayer. I'd have to do some heavy praying myself to get through the next weekend. Not going to Spinster's Spree two years in a row was nothing. But finding out my one secret love hadn't waited for me—that hurt!

As for Lissa, I guess she'd never know why I had needed a doughnut fix this morning. She was in a big hurry to leave now anyway. "Thanks for having me over," she said, waving and dashing down the side aisle.

Interesting, I thought. Maybe Lissa had someone else in mind for Spinster's Spree. . . .

Instead of following my parents into the main aisle, I stood in the pew beside Elton. Actually, I was glad we were alone. "Elton, do you own a Bible?" I asked.

He shook his head no.

I thought for a minute. How could I pull this off without making him feel like a charity case? I thought of the wonderful drawing he'd made of me. The one he'd nearly burned up.

"You gave me a gift," I said. "And I want to give you one. It won't be a loan like the camera. It's something you can keep. Forever."

His eyes started to blink as I told him my plan to purchase a Bible. I didn't say it would take all the money I'd saved for Spinster's Spree. Elton didn't need to know about that.

After he left, I headed down the main aisle to catch up with my family. Seconds later, I heard Jon calling. "Merry, mistress of mirth."

My heart jumped as I turned around. "Hi," I managed to say.

"Hey, Mer." He was smiling. "My silly sis says if Skip's free for Spinster's Spree she's slappin' happy."

Some alliteration! I knew he expected me to come back with a strong reply, but I wasn't in the mood for his word games. "Why don't you just have your sister call him?"

Jon leaned against a pew. "What's wrong?" His eyes grew sober.

"It's nothing." I noticed Ashley inching her way closer. "I better go now," I said, forcing a smile.

"But, Merry?"

"Uh . . . later." I turned on my heels, leaving him in the dust. Served him right. He should've waited for the Word Woman.

ELEVEN

At dinner, I mentioned Jon's sister to Skip. Between mouthfuls, he said Lissa Vyner had already asked him.

I howled. "You're going to the spree with an eighth grader?"

Dad frowned. "Age means little when it comes to love." I waited for his frown to fade. This was a joke, right?

Mom grinned, but Skip nearly choked.

Dad looked over his plate at me. "And what terrific guy will have the honor of our little girl's company this year?"

Doesn't anyone pay attention around here?

"For your information," I blurted, "I stayed home last year."

Dad wore a look of boyish guilt as he turned to face Mom. "I knew that, didn't I, honey?" Poor Dad. Major blunder. Mom nodded, patting his hand.

Skip jumped right in and bailed Dad out. "So who's the lucky guy?" he asked.

"Haven't decided," I said. But it was a cop-out.

Everyone was going to Spinster's Spree. Everyone but me.

After dinner, Dad helped Mom with dishes. I was free to leave and track down Rachel next door. It was Dad's way of saying he was sorry about things. He was cool that way.

Zap 'em Zook was playing volleyball with several other barefoot Amish teens when I showed up. The net stretched high across the side yard, secured between two gray buggies. I hurried past them, hoping to avoid Levi.

"Rachel's in the house," Levi shouted, leaping up to punch the ball. I hurried past his courting buggy. Ignoring it, I headed toward the back door and into the kitchen.

Rachel looked up from a sinkful of dishes and smiled. "*Wilkom,* Merry," she greeted me. "I'll be done here in no time."

Rachel's mother and several other women were wiping the long tables and gathering up trash. To speed things up, I took a cotton towel from the wall hook and dried dishes. I could tell by the mischievous look in Rachel's eye, she couldn't wait to have our secret detective meeting.

It didn't take long for Rachel to get Levi's attention after her chores were finished. She stood at the back door and whistled. I'd forgotten that Rachel had such a powerful pucker. In seconds, Levi dashed over to meet us.

"It's time," Rachel said, glancing mysteriously at me, then at her brother.

Levi smiled in his usual flirtatious way. His grin faded quickly when he noticed Rachel watching him. "Let's go on up in the loft, jah?" he said, pointing to the barn. "It's as good a place as any."

Rachel, also barefooted, followed her brother. I hurried to keep up with them, glancing over my shoulder to see if we were being noticed. By the looks of things, the volleyball game was back in full swing—even several adults had found their way into the game.

The closer I got to the earthen ramp leading to the upper level and the hayloft, the more I felt the excitement. Just walking up the ramp with the smell of soil and cow manure in the air made something warm and tingly drift through my body. Zooks' farm, especially the hayloft, held sweet exhilaration for me.

The smell of dried hay kissed my nose as the three of us entered the secret world. Haylofts were like tree houses—nearly sacred, secluded from the world of grown-ups, and high. Close to heaven.

I sat in the soft hay, leaning back on my hands and feeling the dry, warm ridges push against them. The smells and the atmosphere of this place made me more confident than ever.

Levi sat cross-legged in the hay. Removing his wide-brimmed straw hat, he wiped his forehead as if he were going to say something important. His white, long-sleeved Sunday shirt with black trousers and white suspenders looked the same as the clothes he wore to school and around the farm.

Rachel's white prayer bonnet had slipped cockeyed and she fooled with it while Levi spelled out the game plan.

"I think it's safe to say that Ben Fisher won't be

comin' around here tonight," he said. "There's a singing in our barn till late. And some of the crowds will be coming out for it."

By "crowds," I knew Levi was talking about several different groups of Amish teens in the Lancaster area. Some were rowdier than others.

Rachel's voice sounded pinched. "So you think Ben won't show up tonight?"

Levi picked up a long piece of straw and stuck it in his mouth. "He'd be real dumb if he did."

Behind a cube of hay, a white kitten darted toward us, followed by six or seven more.

"C'mon over, little boy," I said, coaxing the white one.

Rachel laughed. "That one's a girl."

I reached for the tiny barn cat. "What's her name?"

Levi laughed. "We don't name mouse catchers."

"Well, have a good supper, little one," I whispered to the kitten, secretly deciding to name her Lily White. Looking around, I hoped her mousey supper wasn't too close-by.

Rachel was eager to get on with things. Probably because afternoon milking would be starting soon. "We should meet right here tomorrow?"

Levi nodded, making the piece of straw dance between his teeth. "Each one of us can have a lookout post." He pointed to the three spots in the hayloft. "Merry can have the one facing SummerHill Lane away from the house. I'll take the post overlooking the house and yard, and Rachel's spot will be over there." He pointed to the one facing the field. It was the least exciting of the three, but Rachel didn't protest. Following orders made by male family members came naturally to her.

"What'll we do if someone comes prowling around, like, uh, Ben Fisher?" I asked.

Rachel whistled softly. "Can you do that?"

I nodded.

"That will be our signal, then," she said.

"Okay, we're set with a signal, but what about getting help?" I asked.

Rachel smiled. "Levi has all that planned."

"Did ya ever see a man get himself caught up in a lasso?" Levi said.

"Oh no," I said, shaking my head. They weren't kidding, these Zook kids. They had everything planned. Right down to the minute.

Levi stood up. "We'll meet here at dusk tomorrow." Since the Amish didn't wear wristwatches and only went by standard time (even when the rest of us switched to daylight savings), living by landmarks of time, such as dusk, worked well for them.

I glanced at my watch. "When exactly is dusk?"

"You'll know," Rachel said sweetly. "It's when the sun starts going to bed for the night."

Why hadn't I thought of that?

TWELVE

Monday started out fine, except Lissa freaked out on the bus going to school. She must've been having a bad day. "I can't believe what's happening," she said. "I ask Skip to go to Spinster's Spree and he says yes." She sounded horrified.

"What?"

"You heard me, Merry," she said. "Your brother's a senior!"

"I thought you knew that." She was unraveling before my eyes.

"Well, if it hadn't been for one of Jon's older sisters telling her girlfriend and that girl telling her mom, who told my mom," she gasped for air, "things might be cool. But this second, even as we speak, my mom's having a fit about it and I might not get to go."

"Why? Just because Skip's four years older?"

"You should've seen her. I tell you, Merry, my mom's not pretending to be upset about this."

"Well, what do you want me to do?"

She dive-bombed me, nearly hugging me to death. "Oh, thanks, Mer. Would you really?"

"Excuse me?"

She began to plead with me. "If you just talk to my mom, I know it'll change everything."

Honestly, I'd never seen Lissa so wired up.

"You're kidding? You think your mom's gonna listen to me? C'mon, Lissa. I'm his sister, for pete's sake!"

"But she worships you," Lissa insisted.

"Look, Lissa." I lowered my voice and put my head up close to hers. "You have to settle down a little here." I glanced around. In the front of the bus, Chelsea Davis looked like her eyes were about to pop.

Lissa leaned against the back of the seat. She took a deep breath and closed her eyes.

"You okay?" I whispered in her ear.

"I'm fine."

"Good, I'll be right back." With that, I dashed to the seat beside Chelsea.

"What's she moaning about?" Chelsea asked. Sounded like she was having a bad day, too. These things seemed to come in waves.

"It's nothing," I replied.

She poked through her pile of books. "Did you ever find out what happened to that drawing of Elton's?"

"It's mine now," I said. "Elton gave it back to me the other day." I almost said he nearly burned it up, but I wanted to save that news for the principal. Which is where I was headed first thing, the minute I got off this bus.

"When can I see it?" she asked.

"What for?"

"Just curious." I had no idea what she was getting at.

I turned around to check on Lissa, who was staring out the window now, calm and collected.

Chelsea cracked her chewing gum. "Did anyone ever tell you that you overdo it, Merry?"

I turned to face her. "Like how?"

"Like truly this and truly that. Don't you ever get sick of dramatizing everything?" She was acting really weird. "Well, do you?" She was in my face. The smell of her cinnamon gum offended my nose. And her hair—it was an auburn forest.

"I really don't know what's bothering you." And I excused myself and stumbled back down the bus aisle to Lissa.

As soon as I got things squared away at my locker, I rushed to the principal's office to make an emergency appointment. When Mr. Lowry was finally available, I tried to talk sense to him about why Elton Keel, gentleman and docile human being, would want to purposely get himself suspended.

"Elton's not a firebug," I insisted. "He merely took his frustrations out on this picture." I pulled it out of my notebook. "See this? It's truly a masterpiece. How could an insensitive firebug create something so wonderful?"

Mr. Lowry surveyed the charred drawing.

"I only wish I hadn't been so insensitive," I continued. "If I had held on to this in the first place, none of this with Elton would've happened. Don't you see, sir, it's a self-esteem problem. Plain and simple. It's mostly my fault that he's not in school today."

Mr. Lowry's crinkly eyes narrowed into slits as he steered his gaze away from the drawing and back to me.

"You are absolutely right about this young man's talents, Merry. And I'd be delighted to offer leniency in this matter, but rules are rules, and your friend will have to wait out his suspension." He stood up and leaned on his desk. "I'm very sorry." His eyes popped open.

Reluctantly, I stood up, waiting for him to return the sketch. Hoping he'd catch the hint, I stared at the hand that held the drawing. Finally, I just plain asked him for it. "Uh, if you don't mind, I'd like to have that back."

Someone behind me snickered. I spun around. It was Cody Gower sporting a sly grin. My throat turned to cotton. How long had he been standing there?

"That's a reasonable request," Mr. Lowry spouted, motioning Cody in while he dangled Elton's drawing between his thumb and pointer finger. Like it was contaminated or something. "On second thought, I think I'll keep this in Elton's file for the time being."

My heart sank.

The purpose in visiting the principal today was to try to help Elton. But by the solemn look on Mr. Lowry's face, it appeared that I may have made things worse.

❧   ❧

By third period class, everyone in school had heard the rumor. *Merry Hanson was in love with a retard.*

"Is it true?" Lissa asked as I deposited my books at my locker.

"What?"

She gave me a penetrating look. "You have been awfully nice to Elton lately, loaning him your camera and—"

"Christians are supposed to be nice," I said.

I noticed Lissa's eyes. They were disapproving, and when she spoke again her voice sounded breathy and nervous. "You can tell me anything, Mer. We're friends, right?"

I shrugged. "Sure."

"Well?"

"What's the point?" I punctuated my words with the slam of my locker. "Spreading rumors of this magnitude is a very guy thing to do."

"Oh, so you're saying it's not true."

"Bingo!" And with that realization, Lissa's face burst into a bubble gum smile and she scampered off to class, looking downright relieved.

Even Chelsea cornered me after school. Rumors get moldy with age. As far as I was concerned, the comments floating around school weren't worth repeating, and I told her so.

"Just drop it," I said, feeling a deeper emotion than simple anger as I stood watching her peer into her locker mirror. I was worried for Elton. Really worried.

There had to be a way to stop this nonsense before Thursday. I couldn't stand the thought of him returning to school, only to experience Cody Gower's pathetic jokes.

Outside the building, I waited for the bus, ignoring whispers and the catty looks of several girls. Important things were on my mind. More important than dealing with so-called friends and their rumor-laden second guessing. Tonight at dusk I would turn detective. Spending the evening spying with my Amish friends would be a refreshing change from this truly ridiculous day. Whether or not we caught Ben Fisher at his tricks didn't matter. I needed a break from the modern world!

THIRTEEN

The bus dropped me off at the willow grove. Standard procedure. Only today, something was different. Elton's bike was parked a short distance off the road.

The bus lurched forward, spewing exhaust fumes in my face. I held my breath till the fumes dissipated, then I let my eyes comb the trees in search of Elton.

It wasn't long till I spotted him, down in a hollowed out place nearly hidden from the road. The spot had been one of Faithie's and my favorites.

Elton was holding my Polaroid, aiming at the Zooks' barn. Watching him use the camera made me feel good about my decision to loan it out. As I watched him from afar, the frustration of the day began to seep away. Elton was making good use of his time away from school. Making the best of an unfortunate situation.

I admired him for that.

Slowly, I headed into the grove toward the thickest part, delighted that Elton had returned. What a truly beautiful way to spend the afternoon—with a camera and sketch pad.

Not wanting to startle him, I stood back a few feet

from where he sat in the grassy hollow.

Click. He took a picture and let the camera rest beside him.

"Hi," I said as he turned around. "Looks like you're hard at work."

Eltòn's eyes twinkled.

"Doing another drawing of Zooks' barn?"

A faint blush of color crept into his face. He shook his head no.

"What then?" I asked. "Your first picture of the barn was incredible. There's no way you can improve on it."

He put his hand on his heart, as if to thank me. Then he picked up the instant picture and handed it to me.

"Oh, you're drawing cows today?"

He nodded.

"That's something I've never tried." I handed the picture back, wondering if I should tell him about my encounter with the principal today.

Then, out of the secret stillness came the sound of bare feet pounding the earth. I whirled around to see Rachel coming toward me. She was out of breath. "Merry, come quick!"

"What is it?"

She grabbed my arm. "Levi wants us to meet in the hayloft before Dat and Mam get back from the bishop's."

"Why, what's happened?"

"Ach, nothing to worry much about," she said.

"Well, it must be something," I persisted.

I could tell that Rachel was bashful about talking in front of Elton.

"I'm sorry," I said to him. "This is Rachel Zook, my

friend, and I have to go with her for a little bit. I'll see you later, okay?"

The corner of his mouth began to twitch, and he put his right hand up in front of him, as though he wanted to wave.

I ran with Rachel out of the willows and toward the pasture, glancing back as we crawled over the picket fence. Elton was still fooling with my camera the last I saw him.

Rachel started talking. "Mam and Dat went to some doings at the bishop's. Levi says it's about Ben Fisher, but we can't be sure. Anyhow, Levi wants us to go over our spying plans one more time before tonight, while no one's home."

"Good idea." I matched my stride with hers. "Maybe Ben'll repent at the meeting and you won't have to worry."

"For his sake, I hope so." She cast a furtive glance my way; her lower lip trembled. "Shunning's the last thing a body wants." And I believed her.

By the time we ran up the barn ramp and into the hayloft, I was gasping for air. I dove into the sweet, sweet hay, my heart pounding in my ears.

"We probably don't have more than an hour before everyone gets back home," Levi explained. He closed and latched the heavy double doors, making the loft darker and more secretive. Then he began rehearsing our plans from yesterday. "Maybe we should practice hiding at our lookouts."

"Yes, let's!" Rachel shouted with glee as though this were a game.

Levi tweaked a piece of straw and put it in his mouth. "Okay, we'll have a practice. Everyone just pretend it's dusk. Now . . . sneak into the barn and take your post quietly." He lowered his voice. "Tonight when we all meet, Mam and Dat, Grossdawdy and Grossmutter will be in the house. They mustn't know we are out here."

At that moment, the tiny white kitten crept out of hiding, coming over to me. "How will you and Rachel be able to sneak out without your parents suspecting something?" I asked, picking up Lily White.

"We'll think of a way," Levi said. And it struck me that he must've done some late night sneaking before.

"Where's the lasso?"

Levi smiled. "I have it all ready." I knew better than to ask where. Amish boys were taught to model their fathers. And in Levi's case, it was obvious that he'd picked up the influential, take-charge voice of stern Abe Zook.

"Don't forget to whistle." Rachel leaned back in the hay, resting her head on her hands.

"Can we practice now?" I asked.

"If you want to," Levi said. "Just don't whistle too loud."

I puckered up my lips and forced the air gently through. Easy enough.

"Shhh!" Rachel cocked her head. "I hear something."

Levi's eyes were saucers. "Ach! What do ya hear?"

"I'm not sure. Sounds like a car."

Levi shook his head. He was crouched in the middle of the hayloft. "No cars."

"Listen!" Rachel insisted. I wondered who on earth would be driving a car onto Zooks' property.

96

Levi dashed to the window in the gabled end of the upper level. It was across from the hayloft on the opposite side of the barn. Levi's courting buggy and farm equipment were kept there. He leaped up on his buggy, gazing out the window.

"See anything?" Rachel asked.

Levi shook his head. "Nothing's out there. But we're gonna be ready if Ben—or whoever it is—shows up come dusk."

"Shouldn't we have a signal besides a whistle?" I asked. "I mean, what if we see someone and freak out, and we're too scared to pucker?"

Levi jumped off the buggy and ran alongside the wall as he made his way back to the hayloft. "If I see something, I'll whistle. Then you distract him, Rachel, with your horse sounds."

Rachel agreed, but this horse stuff was news to me. I'd never known Rachel to make horse sounds. Ever.

That's the thing about friendship: someone's always changing.

The spying rehearsal began. Rachel climbed up on a feed bin filled with loose hay—her post overlooking the field. Levi marched back to his window view of the house and yard. I settled down at my perch on a bale of hay, snuggling Lily White as I watched for intruders. The moment was soft and peaceful, and I took advantage of it by breathing in the sweet, penetrating aroma of horses and barn.

After a few minutes, Levi called to us. "Okay, time's up. Good enough for now."

He was jumping off his precious buggy when one of

the horses below us began to whinny. Another horse, and another, joined in the chorus and the neighing grew to a terrifying pitch. I heard the unmistakable sound of horses kicking at the stalls, trying to escape. Lily White arched her back and let out an ear-piercing "Me-e-ow!"

"What do ya hear, little lady?" I said as she leaped off my lap. Worried, I glanced around at the shadowy haylofts. Who was scaring the horses?

Levi whistled softly and I looked at him. For one eternal second our eyes locked in powerful recognition. This was no longer a practice run. This was the real thing!

Levi grabbed the rope and made a running leap. I knew what he was up to. He suspected someone was on the ground level irritating the livestock. Maybe Ben Fisher!

Clinging to the rope, Levi swung out past the loft, into the open area between the loft and the gabled end.

"See anything?" I peered over the edge.

Levi's face turned white.

"Smell that?" Rachel whispered.

I sniffed the air. Gasoline fumes!

My stomach wrenched into a cold knot.

FOURTEEN

Levi came flying back on the rope. "Get out of the barn! Fast!"

Then he did a frightful thing. Taking a running leap, Levi swung out over the second floor opening again and let go of the rope, disappearing below.

A half second later, he was shouting, "Fire! Fire! The barn is burning!"

I grabbed Rachel's hand and ran toward the closed double barn doors. Halfway across the loft, Rachel stumbled and fell. "Hurry! Get up!" I pulled on her hand.

A black ball of fire shot through a small opening in the loft floor. I screamed as the flames licked at her bare foot. Stunned, Rachel's face turned beet red as she clutched her right foot. With my help, she managed to hop one-legged across the loft. We came to the locked double doors and I struggled with the latch.

Smoke from smoldering bales of hay burned my eyes. Frantically, I shoved on the heavy wooden latch.

Stuck!

I tried again and again, fear pulsing through me. Billowing smoke filled the barn as the fire spread.

I leaned hard against the latch. Finally, it popped opened. With one giant heave, I shoved the barn doors wide. "Thank you, Lord!" I shouted, helping Rachel down the dirt ramp leading to the open field below. She hobbled on one leg, leaning hard against me. At last, we were safe—away from the burning barn.

Levi emerged out of the smoky ground level at the other end of the barn, sputtering and coughing as he led the mules out. Six beautiful Belgian horses followed. Working quickly, Levi secured the animals a safe distance away. By now the barn was sending up a spiral of raging, black smoke.

"Rachel's hurt!" I called, and Levi came running to inspect her blistered foot.

"It's burnt just a little," he said. "Get some cold water on it right away." He patted her shoulder. Then with a hopeless glance at his father's barn, he shook his head, wiping his sooty face. "I'll go get help."

"It's useless," Rachel said, still holding her red foot as she hobbled toward the outside pump well. "The ole barn'll be gone in minutes." Levi ignored her comment and ran to the house.

"Where's he going?" I asked.

"To ring the bell on the back porch," she said. "It will bring help."

I helped Rachel to the pump, then looked back at the blazing fire, thankful to be alive. That's when I spotted the white kitten perched high on the barn's window ledge.

Lily White!

Without a second thought, I left Rachel and ran toward the bank of earth leading to the barn's second story.

"No, Merry! Come back!" Rachel called. "It's not safe!"

Peering inside, I could see the kitten. For some reason she'd chosen my lookout post. "Here, kitty, kitty," I coaxed her with my best kitty-lovin' voice. I had to get her out of there. Fast!

"Merry!" Rachel was hysterical. "Forget about the cat. Come back!"

For a split second I thought of leaving the kitten behind, but through the haze of smoke, I saw her tremble. I couldn't do it. I just couldn't leave her to die a fiery death.

I eyeballed the distance between Lily White and myself, calculating the amount of time it would take. I could make it. I was sure of it . . . if I hurried.

"Merry!" Rachel wailed from the yard below. "Please don't!"

Taking a deep breath, I darted into the loft. The air around me penetrated the pores of my skin like an instant sunburn as I made my way to the window. I thought my cheeks would melt as I climbed the bales of hay, stretching . . . reaching for the darling kitten.

Just when I thought my lungs would burst, I exhaled and took in a quick breath. Smoke! It burned my lungs and made me cough uncontrollably. My eyes teared up.

Zooks' bell began to toll.

In a flash, I snatched the white fur ball off the ledge and slipped her into the bib part of my overalls. A spray of crackling fire exploded below as I crept around the wall side of the loft. At the opposite end, Levi's courting buggy writhed and twisted in the blazing inferno. And for one second, I regretted never having taken a ride in it.

The heat made my scalp burn, but I kept going, making my way toward the open double doors. Lily White meowed and trembled inside my overalls. She dug her razor-claws into my chest. The pain took my breath away, and I sucked in more dangerous smoke.

Suddenly, a wall of fire, like a volcanic eruption, spewed out of the opening below. I screamed as it rolled toward me, blocking my way of escape. I reeled back in terror.

My brain clouded up. I couldn't decide which way to go. The heat . . . the fear paralyzed me.

Precious seconds ticked away.

Ding-a-dong! Ding-a-dong! Ding-a—

Zooks' bell continued its dreadful tolling.

Was I going to die?

In one last desperate move, I yanked a tarp off a rusty old push mower and covered myself. The insulation made a difference, and I began to grope my way to the door.

Then something knocked me off balance. A white light went off in my head and I fell backward into the hay.

Lily White shook hard and I held her close. She was safe . . . riding in a courting buggy . . . Lily White . . . dressed in a white fur coat . . . on a hot day . . . too hot . . .

Fighting the haze in my mind, I heard a voice. Harsh. Grating. High-pitched. It mingled with the sound of a distant bell.

"Merr-ry-y!"

The voice rang out again. And again. Like the Zooks' bell, it tolled its message.

"Merr-ry-y!"

Like the monotonous ticking of a clock.

"Merr-ry-y!"

Part of me tried to step away from the blackness and survey the situation. And as if in a dream, that part of me recognized the voice.

It was *his* voice. The voice no one had ever heard. And it was coming closer!

I tried to rouse myself to answer his call. Afraid that I might never answer it. Ever again. Then, with every fiber of my being, I listened . . .

And heard nothing.

FIFTEEN

I was vaguely aware of someone carrying me away from the heat. My arms dangled; legs flopped. The tarp slipped to the ground.

Welcome fresh air rushed over me. I coughed, almost choking. Seconds passed and I became aware of strong arms lifting me down to the ground. The cool blades of grass came through my shirt making me shiver. I felt my eyelids flutter. Slowly, I opened them.

A cherub face looked down at mine. An innocent face, with eyes full of pain.

"Elton?" I heard myself say.

He nodded and didn't stop. Not until I reached up and touched his face. Most of his hair was gone. His beautiful blond hair had been singed off by the fire's fury. In its place were burns and blisters. At that moment, even in spite of my terrible confusion, it all made sense. Elton had saved my life.

"Thank you," I whispered. "Thank you."

Before he could respond, two men in white rushed over and had him lie down. In the midst of my fog, I heard them calling for two stretchers.

"He doesn't talk," I said softly as gentle hands inspected my body. But my words were too soft for anyone to hear, and there was no energy left in me to repeat them.

For the first time, I was aware of the crowd. I turned my head to see fire engines, police cars, and an ambulance. Huge plumes of black smoke billowed out over the area. Two paramedics placed me on a stretcher and I felt myself being wafted through space toward an ambulance.

"Merry!" It was Levi's voice. He was running alongside the stretcher, looking down at me, his straw hat gone. "What happened? I thought you were safe at the pump . . . with Rachel."

"Don't excite her," one of the paramedics said. "She's in shock."

"Where's Lily?" I muttered. But before Levi could answer, I was lifted into the ambulance. The doors closed and the shrill siren settled into the mosaic of patterns and sounds in my mind.

Questions came, but I was too weary, too dizzy, to ask them. I let my body relax as we sped away. . . .

✢   ✢

When I awoke, shadows played tricks with my vision. Where was I? The smell of antiseptic tickled my nose.

"Honeybunch?" It was Dad's voice.

I opened my eyes again. Mom and Dad were leaning over my hospital bed. Dad held my hand. "Hello, baby," he said.

I yawned, still wiped out from the ordeal.

"Feeling better?" Mom asked.

"I guess." The words tiptoed out.

She smiled. "This isn't an ideal way to get out of going to school, you know."

Skip poked his head between them. "Welcome back, Mer. Heard you saved a cat." He held up the white kitten for me to see.

"Lily," I whispered, reaching for her.

Skip held her in his cupped hand. "She lost a little hair, but she'll be fine."

Maybe it was the mention of hair, but suddenly I remembered. "Is Elton okay?"

Dad squeezed my hand. "The young man who carried you out of the barn is being treated for smoke inhalation and second-degree burns. He'll be spending the night here, too." He glanced at Skip. "Your brother told us about your new friend."

Even in spite of the haze in my brain, I knew that I could trust whatever Skip had said about Elton.

"He saved our baby's life," Mom cooed.

"Where *is* Elton?" I asked, trying to sit up.

"Two rooms down," Dad said.

Skip piped up. "Yeah, and if you're a good little Merry, tomorrow I'll wheel you over to visit him."

"Tomorrow?" I said, leaning back on the pillow. "What's tomorrow?"

Mom smoothed my hair gently. "Tomorrow is Tuesday, pumpkin. And the docs say you'll be coming home."

I drifted in and out, hearing them, yet not hearing them . . . so much talk of the amazing thing Elton had done. Risking his life for me. Burns . . . guardian angels . . . a miraculous escape.

Their muffled voices rose and fell, then completely

disappeared. And I fell into a deep sleep.

❧　❧

Elton was sitting up in bed having breakfast the next day when Skip and I went to visit. I hadn't needed a wheelchair like Skip suggested. I walked down the hall on my own just fine.

Elton wore a porous white bandage on his head. I could tell by the way he sat, straight and stiff, that he was in pain. Tears blurred my vision as I looked at his hands and forearms. They too had been wrapped with sterile nonstick dressing to protect his burns and keep the air out.

A plump, older woman stood over him, holding a cup of apple juice to his lips. "Hello, there." Her face broke into a wide smile as I came in.

Who is she? Then I noticed the striking resemblance between her and my friend.

"How's Elton doing?" I asked.

"Oh, he's doing just fine, just fine." She tucked a handkerchief under the waistband of her gathered skirt. "I'm Winnie Keel, Elton's grandma. And you must be Merry." She extended her hand to shake mine. "Call me Grandma Winnie."

I turned to introduce Skip. "This is my brother, Skip."

"How do you do, young man," Grandma Winnie said cheerfully.

I inched closer to Elton's hospital bed, which was cranked up too high. If I could just see his eyes . . .

"I . . . I'd like to talk to Elton," I said hesitantly. "Is that okay?"

"Oh, no bother," she said, lowering the bed a bit. Then, pulling her hankie out of its hiding place, she waved it, grinning from ear to ear.

When she and Skip had gone, Elton struggled to pick up his pen from the breakfast tray. He held it in midair, staring at it as though he wished he could click it.

"Here," I said, reaching over and taking the pen. "Your hands are too hurt for that." And I began clicking away.

On and off.

On . . . off.

I didn't feel one bit silly about clicking Elton's pen for him. In fact, I clicked it for about two minutes before I stopped. "I can't remember if I thanked you last night," I said.

He nodded.

"Everything's so blurry from yesterday. Maybe you feel the same way."

He seemed to understand as he nodded.

I thought about the fire and the way he'd called my name over and over. "I . . . I heard you, Elton. I heard your voice."

He pursed his lips, forming what looked like the beginning of an *M*. He tried again—this time his face turned red with the effort. But there was no sound in him.

"It's all right," I whispered.

He stared down at his breakfast tray, motionless. I looked at his head, wrapped in sterile bandages, and held my breath to keep from sobbing. Here sat a true friend.

Elton had done a heroic deed for only one reason. Friendship. A powerful word for a kid who couldn't say it. And even more special for a kid who'd never experienced it. Until now.

A light tapping came at the door. I expected to see Skip, or maybe Elton's grandma, but it was a nurse leading two policemen into the room.

What are they doing here? I thought.

"You'll have to excuse us," one of the cops said. "We have a few questions to ask Mister Elton Keel." I didn't like the way he leaned on the word "mister."

Worried, but not protesting, I said goodbye to Elton, and the nurse escorted me out of the room. "Be sure and tell them he can't talk," I pleaded with the nurse. "Please?"

She smiled, assuring me that she would.

In a few minutes, Skip showed up sporting a sub sandwich. I begged him to stand outside Elton's room and listen in on the conversation with the cops.

"What for?" He bit into his sandwich.

"Please, just do it?" Miraculously, he went without an argument.

In a few minutes, Skip returned looking totally surprised. He sat down in the gray vinyl chair next to my bed.

"What did you hear?" I propped myself up with two pillows.

"You don't wanna know."

I gasped. "What are you saying?"

He leaned forward, resting his arms on his legs, studying me. "This might upset you, Mer."

"What? I can handle it. Just tell me."

He took a deep breath. "The cops think Elton had something to do with the barn fire."

"How can they say that?"

Skip stared at his feet. "Two of the cops remembered Elton from the fire at your school."

"Elton's not a firebug!" I swung my feet over the side of the bed, as though scooting to that position would make what I had to say more powerful. "You have to make them understand, Skip. You have to!"

Skip stood up. "I barely know this Elton person."

"He's not 'this Elton person,' " I shot back. "You sound like you hate him or something."

"You've got it all wrong, Mer. I think you better get ready to check out of the hospital. Dad and Mom'll be here any second." He looked at his wristwatch.

"That's just great! Change the subject, why don't you."

Skip turned and left the room in a huff.

I muttered to myself. "Dad's a doctor; maybe he can talk sense to those crazy cops."

Suddenly, Skip poked his head back into my room. "You're not thinking clearly, Mer. The police have no other suspects, and they do have reason to think that Elton was involved . . . so why shouldn't they question him?"

"How on earth do they expect to get answers out of him when he doesn't talk?" The whole thing was so ridiculous.

Skip tossed his sandwich wrapper in the trash.

"Hey, what about Ben Fisher?" I asked. "Where was

he when the Zooks' barn burned?"

"I don't think you can pin this on Ben. Besides, no one saw him anywhere near the Zooks' place yesterday. But Elton Keel, well . . . he was right there."

I fought back the tears. "Elton wouldn't go to all the trouble to start a fire and then rescue me from it," I said. "He's not totally ignorant, like you think."

"C'mon, Merry. That's not fair." And with that, Skip left the room for good.

If the nurse hadn't come in, I might've cut loose and bawled. She changed the dressing on my arms, reapplying the soothing cream to my burns. "You'll want to keep these areas as dry as possible for several days," she said. "Be sure to put this cream on and change the dressing daily."

"Thanks," I said, but my mind was on Skip's words. *The police have no other suspects.*

I gathered up my things, waiting for the doctor to check me out. Actually, I was too sick to go anywhere, and it wasn't from the lousy arm burns either. The police made me furious. How could they just go and charge Elton with something he hadn't done? Had they forgotten what he *had* done?

How many of them would risk their lives—charge into a burning barn—to save another human being?

Elton was innocent. One hundred and ten percent, amen. And I was going to clear his name!

SIXTEEN

That afternoon, instead of going home with Grandma Winnie, Elton was hauled off to Maple Springs, a juvenile detention center. He would stay there until his hearing came up in a few days.

"The Zooks haven't pressed charges," Dad explained at supper.

"Then why's Elton in jail?" I wailed.

"It's not jail," Dad said. "Not even close."

"I'm sure it feels like it," I muttered. "He doesn't belong there." Visions of Elton sitting high in the old oak tree near Hunsecker's Mill Bridge haunted me. He needed to be outdoors in touch with nature, not in some dark holding place for delinquents.

"The district attorney pressed charges, Merry," Mom said, offering me some more noodles. "Arson is very serious business."

"But Elton didn't do it!"

Dad cut into his meatloaf, taking a bite and swallowing before he spoke again. "Remember the fire at your school, Merry? You told me yourself why Elton started it."

"He was just mad . . . uh, hurt, really."

"And why was that?"

"Because I rejected his picture. But this isn't like that. Elton's not a firebug!"

Dad looked over at Mom and back at me. "Elton set fire to his picture of you, only to retrieve it before it burned." He took a deep breath. "I think there may be a parallel here, honey."

"You can't possibly believe that he torched the barn so he could save me." It made no sense.

Dad was silent.

"C'mon, Dad, can't you at least talk to the police about his good side? I mean, what about the fact that he saved my life? Doesn't that count for anything?"

"I'm very certain the police are aware of that," he said in his most professional voice. "I think we should take a few steps back from this thing emotionally"—and here he stared at me hard—"and let the legal system do its work."

I stared at the kitchen wallpaper, tracing the strawberry vines with my eyes. Dad was beginning to sound like a shrink or something. Whose side was he on anyway?

After supper, I fed my cats. Four of them. Lily White seemed to fit right in with the three Hebrew children. Abednego was the only one who'd exhibited the least bit of jealousy. Shadrach and Meshach actually seemed to like her.

Lily White's singed fur conjured up scenes of Nebuchadnezzar's fiery furnace in the book of Daniel. The white color of her coat reminded me of the angel of the Lord, who walked with the three boys in the king's furnace. I smiled as I watched Lily White eat her tuna delight. An angel must've been with Elton and me during the barn fire. Only we didn't get to see it like King Neb- uchadnezzar had. Maybe it was just as well.

I went to my room and threw myself on the bed, star- ing at the ceiling. Mom and Dad didn't understand. And it was truly horrible. The very people who you'd think would help at a time like this . . . and all they could do was talk about the legal system.

Several hours later, Mom knocked on my door, asking to come in. I wasn't in the mood for company, so she left me alone, which is exactly what I needed.

I rolled over and turned the radio on. Sometimes mu- sic helped when I was like this. That, and talking to God. But today I was too angry to pray. Pulling the pillows out from under my head, I went over the events of the week, thinking through the days since last Thursday when I'd accidentally taken Elton's picture at school.

Tons of things had happened in five days. That thing with Cody Gower in art. The lunchroom scene. Elton's suspension from school. The Zooks' fire. And now this.

I stared at the wall where my finest photography hung on display. Not a single picture was of a person. I didn't take shots of people. Places and things had always inter- ested me more.

The moment in the hall last Thursday had come as a big surprise for Elton. I could still see his arms going up over his face, cowering away from the flash. But the en- counter with Elton—bumping into his life the way I had—*that* had come as a bigger surprise to me.

It seemed strange to think that there was actually a picture of a human being in my undeveloped roll of film.

I smiled thinking about it. Most definitely a first. Maybe, by God's providence, it hadn't been an accident after all.

I sat up, looking at my arms. How much more they might've been burned—or worse—if Elton hadn't come when he did. It made me wonder where his picture fit in my gallery of photos. In my gallery of life . . .

It was late when I asked Mom to help me change the dressing on my arms. I didn't really need her help, but she probably needed to know I wanted it.

❧   ❧

I didn't go to school on Wednesday. Mom wanted me to stay home. And it was a good thing, too. The extra day would give me plenty of time to go and visit Miss Spindler—Old Hawk Eyes. She made it her duty to keep close tabs on things in the neighborhood. People thought she had a high-powered telescope or something. How else did she know about everything and everyone?

Miss Spindler was still wearing a terrycloth bathrobe and slippers when she answered the door. "Well, my dear, how's every little thing?" She eyed the bandages on my arms.

"Well, you probably know about the Zooks' fire," I said, "and how I got out alive. So I won't bore you with all that."

"Oh my, dearie, 'tis not a bore." She cackled as if she couldn't wait to hear my version.

I began to tell her about Elton and how he'd risked his life for mine. Pausing, I took a deep breath before asking the question burning inside me. "Miss Spindler, is there any chance you saw someone prowling around on Zooks' farm Monday afternoon . . . around three?"

She cocked her head. "Uh, what time did you say?"

"Three o'clock," I repeated.

A smile burst across her wrinkled face. "Well, my dear, I must tell you that between three and four each and every weekday, the world comes to a screechin' halt."

I had no idea what she was referring to. "Why's that?" I asked.

She pointed a long, bony finger at her television. "That's the reason I didn't see nobody on Zooks' farm, dearie."

"Oh, you have a favorite show or something?"

"You heard right."

I stood up to go, disappointed with this lack of news. "It's just too bad about Elton," I said, under my breath.

She leaped up suddenly. "Now what is this wide world coming to!" she exclaimed, nearly scaring me to death. "Oddballs like that Elton fella oughta be put away. For good."

"Excuse me?" I couldn't believe my ears.

"That's right," she said, waving her hands through the air. "I've heard about retard people. You just can't be too careful."

"He saved my life!"

"That's all well and good, but the thing is, the boy's trouble. Powerful big trouble." She sighed. "Why else would the police go and lock him up?"

"I'm sorry, Miss Spindler, but I have to go now." I marched straight to the front door, and just like that, I left. People like Old Hawk Eyes should have to spend one hour with someone as sensitive and kind as Elton Keel.

Then they'd know exactly what this wide world was coming to!

On the way back to my house, I noticed a bunch of buggies parked at the Zooks'. Amish friends and neighbors were clearing away debris from the barn fire. Tomorrow, the new foundation would be laid for a new one. That's the way it was with the Amish. Instead of buying insurance, everyone worked together to rebuild. In the plain community, that's all the insurance they needed.

After lunch, the mail came. There was a card for me from Jonathan Klein. He'd written the verse himself.

> *Get well, won'tcha? Mistress Merry of mirth must make monumental effort to match wits with the Word Wizard. Can't compete without clever company, comprende?*
> *Just Jon*

I smiled and read it again. The Alliteration Wizard had come through with a cool get-well card, and Spinster's Spree or not, I couldn't imagine him sharing our private game with anyone else. Especially not Ashley Horton!

Later that afternoon, Mom announced that she had a few errands to run. "Need anything, Mer?"

"Will you pick out a Bible for Elton at the Christian bookstore?" I asked.

Mom agreed, and I ran upstairs to get the money I'd saved for Spinster's Spree.

"Now be sure to rest while the house is quiet." She blew a kiss as she left.

A nap would feel good. But before lying down, I got the brilliant idea to call Lissa's father. Since he was one of the cops at the school the day of the trash-can fire, and because I was a friend of his daughter, maybe I could get him to see the light about Elton.

Lily White followed me into Dad's study. She was fast becoming my shadow. After dialing the police department, I waited for the dispatcher to connect me with Officer Vyner. Several recordings later, he came on the line.

"Hello, this is Merry Hanson, Lissa's friend."

"Yes, Merry, how can I help?"

I explained the reasoning behind my view that Elton was innocent. "He should be set free," I insisted. "He didn't start the fire."

"I understand how you must feel," Lissa's father said, "but Elton is a very unstable person. He is autistic."

There was that word again. Autistic. Skip had used it offhand to describe Elton last week.

"But that doesn't mean he's destructive," I said. "Elton is a very sensitive person. I wish you could get to know him."

"I'm sure you've seen a side of Elton that the police force hasn't," he said kindly, "but unless you can provide something more substantial than your feelings, I'm afraid Elton will have to be tried for arson."

"What about Ben Fisher? He's been causing all sorts of trouble at the Zooks'. Have you talked to him?" I felt bad about breaking my promise to Rachel, but I had to help Elton now.

"We've heard some stories flying around, but nothing we can confirm, Merry. You know the Amish won't implicate one of their own." I heard his beeper going off like crazy in the background. "Substantial evidence is what we need."

"Thanks for your time, sir," I said, and hung up.

I needed proof to clear Elton—just one little thing to get him off the hook. It sounded so easy. Maybe a bike ride past Ben Fisher's place was the answer. Maybe I'd even get brave and talk to Ben myself.

SEVENTEEN

The bike ride turned up absolutely nothing. I even went up to the Fishers' farmhouse and asked Ben's mother if I could talk to him.

Anything to get Elton off.

It turned out that Ben was in Ohio, visiting some Mennonite relatives. I didn't think to ask her how long he'd been gone. I was too depressed to think straight.

Finally, I went to my room to rest like Mom wanted. But I never fell asleep. My mind raced ninety miles an hour. The idea that Ben might've been in Ohio on Monday troubled me. Where did that leave Elton?

Lying on my bed, I played with the straps on my camera case. Soon, my cats joined me. They snuggled in as waves of depression poured over me. At long last, I was ready to pray. Sobbing, I told all my fears and concerns to God, asking for His help.

Later, when Mom got home, she came right up to my room. Her hair was windblown, smelling fresh like spring. She ran her fingers through the top of it before opening her shopping bag. She reached inside and pulled out a black leather Bible.

"It's beautiful," I said, stroking the binding.

"When do you plan to give this to Elton?" she asked, looking quite pleased.

"Tomorrow, I think." I wondered if Elton's grandma might agree to meet me at the detention center. "Thanks for getting it, Mom."

She smiled, adjusting the collar on her light blue shirtwaist dress. "You must be plain broke now, Merry," she commented. "But if you need to borrow money for Spinster's Spree, just ask your father."

"Oh, that," I groaned as she walked toward the door. I wanted to forget about Spinster's Spree.

"What, honey?" She turned around.

"Nothing."

Nothing was right.

Mom came over and sat on my bed. Lily White sniffed her hand, checking her out. "Hey, Miss Lily, I've been around here much longer than you have!" Mom said, grinning.

We laughed together. And the lighthearted moment brought welcome relief to the tension of my crazy, mixed-up life.

The next day was Thursday, and while I waited for the school bus, Rachel's sisters came pulling her in a red wagon. She smiled at me from her padded perch, lined with a bright-colored quilt. The girls giggled, their eyes bright and cheeks rosy as they called to me. "Hello, Merry! Are you better?"

I held out my bandaged arms for Nancy, Ella Mae, and little Susie as they gathered close to see. "It still hurts a little, but not too much," I said.

Nancy and Ella Mae held up Rachel's bandaged foot. I leaned over to inspect it. "Can you put weight on it yet?"

Rachel shrugged her shoulders. "Just a little."

I stood up, noticing several gray buggies parked in the Zooks' lane. "Got company?"

Rachel turned to look. "Jah. Jacob Esh and his boys are over deciding things about the new barn with Dat. Jacob is the master carpenter." She turned to look at me. "You hafta come to the barn raising. It's tomorrow, you know."

"I don't know if I should miss school for it, but I'll ask."

Little Susie jumped up and down. "You hafta, Merry. It's so-o much fun!"

Nancy nodded. "Ach, there's more food than you've ever seen."

"Like what?" I said, responding to the eager looks on the girls' faces.

"Like fried ham and gravy, and English walnut pie, that's what!" said Ella Mae.

"Mm-m, sounds good," I said, playing along with the younger girls, rubbing my stomach like Susie.

"Where's Aaron?" I asked, looking around for their nine-year-old brother.

"Oh, he's staying home to help Dat today," Rachel said. "He wants to be a carpenter when he grows up."

"He's lucky," Susie said, rolling her big blue eyes.

"Well, we better get going to school," Rachel said, and her team of sisters pushed and pulled her down the lane.

"Goodbye!" I called.

"Seven sharp," Susie shouted back.

When I finally arrived at Mifflin Middle School, everyone carried on about the fire . . . and me. Even Jon hung around my locker longer than usual. I noticed Ashley Horton get tired of waiting for him and head off to first hour by herself.

At lunch, Chelsea practically hovered. "Let's see what second-degree burns look like," she said. "Is it all blistery and yucky under there?"

Lissa frowned at her across the table. "Don't be gross." She pleaded with me not to take off the bandages.

"Don't worry," I said, glancing at the table where Elton usually sat. It seemed strange that I should notice. After all, I hadn't known him that long. One week today.

Chelsea and Lissa chattered on and on about how they would've died if something horrible had happened to me.

"Did you see your life pass before you?" Lissa said, softly. "That happens to people sometimes."

Chelsea snickered. "You did that for a barn cat?"

I nodded, smiling. "You sound just like my brother."

Lissa sighed. "All I can say is, God must've been watching out for you, Mer."

I waited for Chelsea to freak out about Lissa mentioning God like that. She set her glass of soda down slowly, holding on to it, then looked at me. "Well, someone sure was."

I rejoiced silently. It was a minor breakthrough for a self-declared atheist.

❧   ❧

After school, I sat with Grandma Winnie in the visiting area of Maple Springs. Gooseprickles popped out of my neck as I thought about Elton being stuck there.

"How's Elton today?" I asked his grandma, next to me on the sofa.

"Oh, you know him," she said, waving her hand. "Elton takes things in his stride. I guess you could say he lives his life in his head, so it's hard to take much away from him."

I breathed deeply before asking my next question. "Do you think Elton started the barn fire?"

"He's mighty different, that boy, but setting a barn on fire, well, that's another story."

"So then you think he's innocent."

"Oh, indeed, I do. But it looks as though our hands are tied," she said, her voice drifting off as a counselor led Elton into the room.

Grunting, she pulled herself up off the sofa and shuffled over to Elton. "It's so good to see you, honey-boy." She wrapped her jolly arms around her grandson.

Elton was motionless. And by the blank look on his pale face, I could see he'd regressed quite a bit.

I clenched my teeth, coming to grips with reality. Isolating Elton here, away from the people who loved him, had been a big mistake.

I struggled with my good memories of him—those few times we'd spent in the willow grove and at the covered bridge. Elton had begun to grow, to change. And now . . .

I couldn't bear to see him like this.

Grandma Winnie led him to a chair and he nearly collapsed into it, weak and dejected. I swallowed hard to keep from crying. This special kid, the boy who'd saved my life, needed help.

EIGHTEEN

Elton's grandma stroked his back. "Look who's come to pay you a visit."

I stood up and walked over to him, wishing there was some way I could communicate the important things—how I'd tried desperately to clear his name. I wanted him to know. But the timing didn't seem quite right, especially with Elton's grandma right there—and the counselor breathing down our necks.

"I brought you something." I pulled the gift bag off so he could see the Bible.

He kept staring into space and rocking back and forth, his arms and hands bandaged and limp in his lap.

I thought my heart would break. This was not the same boy who'd sat in church with me, sharing my Bible. And the night he'd stood and clapped at our youth meeting—where was *that* Elton?

His grandma started to talk about the fire, but the counselor intervened. That subject was obviously off limits, and I could see why. Zooks' fire had changed everything.

❧   ❧

That night, after supper, Dad and I had a long talk in his study. He did his best to explain Elton's problem to me. "Autism is a mental disorder, and occurs in two to five of every one hundred thousand live births," he said. "It's found more often in boys than girls." He continued to describe some of the behaviors of autistic people. Elton had nearly all of them.

Everything seemed so complicated, but it was good to know Dad wanted to take time to explain. "There's something else I want to say, Merry," he continued.

"What, Dad?"

"This has to do with your views concerning Elton's innocence." He paused for a moment, scratching his head. "I want you to know I respect your opinion about your friend, and I hope the best for him." He smiled.

"Oh, thank you!" I said, rushing into his arms. Things were so much better now. Finally, Dad was sounding less like the resident shrink, and more like my father.

With little fuss, my parents agreed to let me go to the Zooks' barn raising. "As long as you get your homework assignments finished before Friday," Mom said.

"And please be careful with your arms," Dad said, glancing at the bandages still there.

So it was set. I was looking forward to a frolicking good time, as Susie Zook would say. Frolicking good had its limitations, of course. Tomorrow wouldn't be half as much fun with Elton locked up.

Setting my alarm for six o'clock, I climbed into bed early, wishing and praying that Elton were free. And struggling with what to do to make it happen.

When the alarm sounded the next morning, I was in a deep sleep, dreaming that I was dragging both my cameras through a field. Things were hazy and I tried my best not to stop dreaming, but the alarm clock had done its work. The dream faded away.

Later, I stood in my closet trying to decide what to wear. That's when I remembered my Polaroid camera. I'd loaned it to Elton. Had it burned in the fire? Frustrated about not knowing, I pulled on a lightweight shirt, careful not to disturb the new, clean bandages on my arms. There was really no way to ask Elton about anything these days.

It was full light when I hopped on my bike and rode over to the Zooks. I didn't want to offend my Amish friends by carrying a camera in plain view, so I wrapped it in a paper bag, securing it in my bike basket.

The Old Order Amish didn't allow photographs of themselves. The scriptures about not making any graven images were taken literally.

Abe and Levi were in the field welcoming friends and directing buggy traffic when I arrived. More and more horses and buggies pulled into the yard and parked, lining up all the way to the wagon wheel mailbox at the end of the private lane. Minutes later, a bus came bouncing down SummerHill, packed with Amish men from Strasburg and surrounding areas. They were wearing their work clothes.

By seven sharp, everyone was present—about three hundred Amish folk. Even the Zook grandparents settled into their rocking chairs to sit and watch and visit with the others their age.

Rachel waved when she saw me. "Come on inside, Merry!" She hobbled around on a single, homemade crutch.

I parked my bike near the back door and went into the kitchen. Rachel and her mother were arranging home-made pies and cakes baked by the women whose husbands would build the barn.

Soon the women began stewing chickens for the noon meal. Rachel and I helped fry potato chips with several other women until her mother caught our attention. "Rachel! Merry!" she called. "You girls go and get off your feet now for a while." She shooed us out of the kitchen like flies. Then, turning to her Amish friends, she said, "Ach, that fire was such a terrible fright."

Terrible was putting it mildly, and I thought of Elton again as Nancy and Ella Mae showed up with their little wagon for their big sister. I smoothed out the wrinkles in the quilt and helped Rachel get situated.

"Ask Mam if we can take some angel food cake and cookies with us," Rachel told her sisters.

The girls scampered into the house, letting the screen door slap against the frame. I watched Susie play a game of chase with a friend in the backyard near the old pump. Aaron Zook was hauling tools with a wheelbarrow, help-ing his dad.

I could hear the joking going on among the men as they divided into groups to begin erecting the main tim-bers and frame. It would take sixteen strong men to lift one beam into place.

Nancy and Ella Mae came running with two large pieces of angel food cake and six peanut butter cookies. Nancy handed the plates wrapped with clear plastic to Rachel, who sat like a princess in the wagon.

"That's a very good after-breakfast snack," Rachel said. "Can you bring us some lemonade later on?"

Ella Mae smiled broadly, showing her missing front tooth. "Where are you two going now?"

Rachel looked up at me and I leaned down to pick up the wagon handle. "Merry, where do you want to sit and watch the barn go up?" she asked.

"How about the secret place—in the willow grove?" I suggested. "You girls can come later if you bring us some lemonade," I teased Nancy and Ella Mae.

They giggled and chased each other barefooted as I pulled the wagon over the yard. I stopped to get my camera out of the bike basket before heading down Zooks' bumpy lane to the main road.

"Don't you go hurting your arms pulling me around," Rachel said.

"It's no problem." I turned off SummerHill Lane and headed down the well-worn path to the thickest part of the willow grove. The secret place.

Under the graceful covering of branches and leaves, I spread out the quilt from the wagon and helped Rachel sit down. "How's that?"

"Look at this view we have," she said as I sat beside her on the quilt. She was right—the view was perfect. We could see everything from here.

The men crawled over the beams like ants, working at a feverish pace while Rachel and I talked leisurely about the summer coming up. "My aunt's expecting twins this summer," I said. "In June, I think."

"Twins?" Rachel looked a little surprised. Maybe because she knew Faithie and I had been so close. "You're going to have two new cousins at once."

"That's right," I said. "And my aunt's never had children before and she's deaf."

"Will she hafta teach the little ones how to sign?"

I hadn't thought of that. "I guess so." I reached for the plate with the angel food cake and gave a piece to Rachel. After that, we nibbled on our cookies, soaking up the sun. Feeling lazy and good.

By ten o'clock, it was time for the first break, and we could see all the activity from our vantage point. Women and girls scurried here and there serving sandwiches and doughnuts in baskets to their husbands and fathers. It was a holiday atmosphere, with plenty of laughter and lots of pranks.

After they served Abe and Levi, Nancy and Ella Mae came dashing across the pasture, climbing over the picket fence with tall glasses of cold lemonade splashing out as they came.

"Thanks," I said, taking a sip of the cold drink.

"Anything else?" Nancy curtsied to us, pulling on her black apron, pretending to be our maid.

"No, thank you, not for me," I said. "And you?" I turned to Rachel, playing along.

"I'll have a sandwich, if you please," she said, sounding like a regular English lady.

Ella Mae got the giggles and Nancy challenged her to a race to the picket fence.

I reached for the bag with my camera inside and set up a shot of the quilt and lemonade glasses. "Don't worry, I won't get you in the picture," I promised.

Rachel smiled, trusting me. She leaned over to steady her glass. "That's better."

I stepped back several feet, away from the cozy retreat. Aiming at the quilt, I made the lemonade glasses the focal point.

Click. The picture was done, but something behind Rachel caught my eye. Something red and blue. Something plaid.

I hurried to investigate. When I knelt down, I discovered it was Elton's backpack!

"What did ya find, Merry?" Rachel asked.

Almost reverently, I carried the small plaid backpack over to our quilt. "This belongs to the boy who saved my life," I said softly.

The zipper was open, so I peeked inside. "Oh, look at this." I pulled out my Polaroid camera. "It wasn't burned up after all." A truly happy feeling swept over me.

Rachel peered over my shoulder as I felt around inside the backpack. "What else?"

"Oh, just some pictures he took for an art project," I said, pulling out the developed shots he'd taken.

We looked at Elton's pictures together and Rachel seemed to enjoy them. "There's our old barn," she said, pointing to the silo.

I looked at the next one. It was the same barn. Same silo. Cows grazing peacefully. Martins flying overhead. A car parked in front of the house . . .

"Wait a minute!" I showed Rachel this one. "Look at that!"

Rachel gasped. "Ach, no! That's Ben Fisher's car. What is it doing out in front of our house?"

Quickly, I looked at the next picture. "Who's that walking toward the barn?" My heart was pounding so hard I couldn't see straight.

"Oh, Merry," Rachel said, holding her chest. "It's Ben!" She stared at the picture, squinting. "*Himmel,*" she whispered. "That's a gasoline can."

Our eyes locked.

"Ben Fisher *did* burn down our barn!" she said.

Trembling with relief, I placed my Polaroid and Elton's pictures inside the blue and red backpack. I'd found proof. The proof Officer Vyner needed to clear my friend!

Rachel assured me she'd be okay there in the secret place until I got back. She grinned at me, clapping her hands as I carefully threaded first one bandaged arm, then the next, through the camera strap and Elton's backpack. The scene was something out of my early morning dream.

"Thank you, Lord!" I shouted through the willows. I ran like the wind down the narrow dirt path toward SummerHill Lane. "Thank yo-o-u!"

NINETEEN

Elton didn't nod or shake his head or anything when I asked him later that evening to go to Spinster's Spree with me.

"It's tomorrow at the church, in case you forgot."

He stared straight ahead.

"I'm paying, so you don't have to worry."

His eyes blinked.

Grandma Winnie came out on the porch and sat down, smiling. "Elton's been mighty picky about things since he got home." She leaned next to him, adjusting his head bandage.

"Really? About what?" I asked.

"For instance." She picked up his pen and handed it to her grandson. "He wants to 'talk' about Bible stories all the time."

"That's good," I said. "What's he saying?"

"Just watch," she said as Elton's pen began flying over the sketch pad. A drawing of Adam and Eve began to take shape. They were situated in a beautiful garden. A garden with dense trees; some looked like willows. And there was something else. I watched curiously as he sketched.

Then I saw it. Way in the very back of the garden. "It's a covered bridge!"

Elton's face remained unchanged, but the windows of his soul were shining.

"You've got a great sense of humor," I said, looking right at him. "Maybe you could team up with Anthony the artist from Vermont."

Suddenly, Elton reached over and began thumping on his Bible. I was sure it was his way of saying thank you. Maybe much more.

All the pieces didn't quite fit yet, but I knew the encounter in the hallway at school hadn't been an accident after all. Besides that, there was a roll of film yet to be developed. Film featuring a person. A very special person.

≈   ≈

Ben Fisher was tracked down somewhere in Ohio and brought back for trial. Last I heard, Levi had been going to visit Ben in jail nearly every day. Like I said, Levi was a loyal, true friend.

And Ben repented, too. So he escaped the shunning. Thank goodness!

Lissa talked her mother into letting her go to Spinster's Spree with my brother. In fact, Lissa and Skip, and Elton and I doubled up in Skip's car for the evening. I must admit it wasn't easy pulling Elton into the conversation, but, oh well . . . sometimes silence is golden.

Jon Klein and Ashley Horton experienced a somewhat golden evening as well. In fact, every time I happened to glance over at their table, they were silent.

At the end of the banquet, Elton and I posed for pictures, showing off our matching white bandages. Well, Elton didn't ham it up that much, but at least he got his nodding ritual going again.

I can't decide exactly where that picture—the people picture—will fit on my wall gallery just yet. But it's going up there—no matter what!

Who knows, I might start a new gallery, one featuring windows of the soul. I think it's about time.

From Beverly ... To You

❧   ❧

I'm delighted that you're reading SUMMERHILL SECRETS.
Merry Hanson is such a fascinating character—I can't begin
to count the times I laughed while writing her humorous
scenes. And I must admit, I always cry with her.

Not so long ago, I was Merry's age, growing up in Lancaster County, the home of the Pennsylvania Dutch—my
birthplace. My grandma Buchwalter was Mennonite, as were
many of my mother's aunts, uncles, and cousins. Some of my
school friends were also Mennonite, so my interest and ap-
preciation for the "plain" folk began early.

It is they, the Mennonite and Amish people—farmers, car-
penters, blacksmiths, shopkeepers, quiltmakers, teachers,
schoolchildren, and bed and breakfast owners—who best as-
sisted me with the research for this series. Even though I have
kept their identity private, I am thankful for these wonderfully
honest and helpful friends.

If you want to learn more about Rachel Zook and her people, ask for my Amish bibliography when you write. I'll send
you the book list along with my latest newsletter. Please in-
clude a *self-addressed, stamped envelope* for all correspondence.
Thanks!

Beverly Lewis
℅ Bethany House Publishers
11300 Hampshire Ave. S.
Minneapolis, MN 55438